UPRISING

BURNING SKIES

BOOK 3

CHRIS HARRIS

Published by Vulpine Press in the United Kingdom in 2019

Cover by Claire Wood

ISBN: 978-1-912701-74-2

www.vulpine-press.com

To my beautiful wife Nicky. Thank you for making the world still turn whilst I'm staring at a screen.

CHAPTER ONE

COBRA, DOWNING STREET, LONDON

Adriene Winslet, the Prime Minister of the United Kingdom, sat stunned into silence. The strain of the last weeks, fighting to hold the country together as it rapidly fell into anarchy, showed on her face.

She had been unable to stop the chaos and was reduced to a spectator as her pleas and broadcasts for calm fell on a nation deafened by panic. The police, despite all leave being cancelled and every available officer being sent to the front line, failed to stop the mass outbreaks of public disorder. Shelves in shops and supermarkets were stripped of all goods; the population had been whirled up into a frenzy by the sensationalist-led media that kept fueling anxiety about how soon everyone would starve as food supplies, not just from the USA, but from other countries stopped flowing into UK ports.

The rioting and looting that followed was, in some cases, caused by people's desire to gather as much food as possible by all and any means. But mainly by those in society who realized that they had an opportunity to loot, steal, and destroy property with impunity.

The media, even those outlets which had been fierce supporters, turned on her and her party. Predictions of the imminent outbreak of World War Three further fuelled the fires. No matter how many times she reassured the public and the media, both publicly and privately, that they were doing their utmost to resolve the crisis globally and domestically, she just wasn't believed.

The army had reluctantly—despite protests from every echelon of their hierarchy—been ordered onto the streets to reinforce the dusk-to-dawn curfew that had hurriedly been imposed in an attempt to quell the violence.

The media went apoplectic over this, accusing the government of heavy-handed dictatorial tactics when all the population wanted was to eat. The soldiers, trained for war and not to maintain public order against a population they thought they had enlisted to protect, were not effective anyway and were soon quietly withdrawn following some ugly incidents.

The country needed actions and leadership, but all they had so far from those in power were empty words and promises.

Not that she hadn't tried. Her first instinct was to rush to her old allies, the United States, for help but the apathy and complete unwillingness to get involved she had experienced from other countries had drained her resolve. Most, she suspected, were working hard in the background to secure their positions in the new world order, whatever that was, when it emerged from the terrible destruction and loss of life that the United States had and still was suffering from.

Only Canada and the old traditional enemy Russia were looking at the other path. Both out of self-interest as they shared long borders, one very suddenly and recently, with an adversary that had proved beyond doubt its capabilities and willingness for ruthless action.

Russia had already unleashed a new and unknown weapon against the attackers besieging Cheyenne Mountain. Reports indicated over seven thousand attacking Chinese troops had been killed by this new and terrifying non-collateral damage weapon.

When she had called the Russian president to protest at the action she was left in no uncertain terms that there was no option of sitting on the fence. You were either with them or against them.

She had let her initial muted promises of support quietly slip away when a phone call from China's leader himself, spoken through interpreters, had made her baulk at the consequences he promised would follow if any British involvement was detected against the People's Republic of China.

She justified it to herself that her first priority was to her own people.

Her normally neatly styled hair and manicured image that she portrayed to the public was now ruffled at the edges. Not surprising as the amount of sleep she had been getting since this crisis began could be counted in hours and never more than three in a row.

General Sir Anthony Lloyd, the nation's chief of the defense staff rushed into the room and whispered into the prime minister's ear.

"Can you repeat that again, General? So everyone else can hear," she asked sharply, causing the buzz of noise in the room around her to fall quiet.

The general waited for the last conversations in the room to subside before repeating, "Prime Minister, the Russians and Americans, with the help of Canada, have launched an attack on US soil."

He looked with distain at the prime minister. "Whilst we have sat here, wringing our hands, unable to make a decision for fear of upsetting China, who we all know have committed the biggest act of international piracy ever committed, other countries who can see the bigger picture have chosen to act and not waste time on yellow-livered words of surrender."

Adriene Winslet stood up quickly, real anger showing on her face for the first time, her chair toppling over behind her. "Now look here, General, remember who you are addressing."

The general was sick to his back teeth of the complete lack

of progress the cabinet had made since the crisis started. He had been present at all the COBRA meetings where no will at all had ever been expressed to stand up the international bully and nation stealer that China had turned into.

He could see where this would lead, whereas all the political appointees around the table could only see mediation, reconciliation, and compromise as the way forward.

History, of which he was a student, showed that time and time again nation states who chose the course of action that China had commenced would not stop at just the one victory. One was never enough and whilst their politicians, ambassadors, and emissaries all spread words of peace, rebuilding, and reconciliation, the warmongers and those who pulled the strings in the background would be planning the next move.

One conquest would never be enough.

If China could consolidate their rule and iron grip across what was the most powerful and richest nation on earth in a few short weeks, then no one could stand in their way.

He banged his fist as hard as he could on the table. A crystal decanter toppled over, spilling water across the files and papers scattered across the large polished oak table.

"Ma'am, I think you should also remember who you are addressing. The British Armed Forces are led by the Queen."

He paused and looked around the table before looking the

prime minister straight in the eye.

"But as we all know, as a constitutional monarch she follows the laws and legislations passed by the government in power. Now I can be replaced, and you can find another of my colleagues who may be willing to sit idly by whilst all advice offered is ignored…But as I can be replaced, so can you."

He let that statement settle over the room.

A few looked shocked and worried at the thought of losing positions that had taken a lifetime of work to attain. A few others could not help themselves but glanced at the prime minister, seeing how vulnerable she was and imagining themselves taking over the role.

Having worked up through the ranks of the party herself and knowing how much she had coveted the position, she recognized the few glances thrown in her direction. One vote of 'no confidence' would end her career.

She had fought long and hard to get where she was. Being politically intelligent and shrewd she realized immediately that the next few minutes could be the making, or the ending, of her political life.

After taking a moment to compose herself, she asked the question, "General, you have our attention. Now what do you suggest we do?"

CHAPTER TWO

SAN ANTONIO, TEXAS

General Liu followed the United States Marine Sergeant, still trying to comprehend that he was not his trusted aide Sergeant Huang, but an enemy spy. A spy who nevertheless had just saved him from a firing squad. He followed him silently as the two of them ran through the basement and service areas of the hotel that he had been imprisoned in by Agent Fen Shu following his arrest the day before.

"Where are you taking me, Hua—?" He stopped himself before he called his savior by his pseudonym as he paused at a corner. The sergeant checked the way ahead was clear then waved him on.

"Sir, I am taking you out of the city. After that I have no more information."

Liu nodded and asked no more questions. His mind was too busy trying to compute the last five minutes of his life to go through the many permutations of what may lie ahead.

He was officially an enemy of his beloved homeland. Sentenced to death for crimes against the state. He knew the allegations made against him were false. Made up by Fen Shu after he continually criticized her badly thought-out and executed plan to invade and control the US.

He knew if victory was to be claimed, the only way it could be achieved would be by winning over the local population, not by force and intimidation, but through hearts and minds.

Most of the citizens of the United States had been under the impression that the Chinese had arrived to render assistance following crippling attacks by an unknown party. That lie was seen through the moment the camps were set up and tens of thousands were herded into them and forced to live in squalid conditions, not as grateful survivors, but as prisoners.

Word soon spread, and the beginnings of a resistance began.

He'd tried to tell her that the camps were strategic mistakes taking up valuable resources and manpower. Resources that anyone as well versed as he was in military planning would know would be better used in securing the victory that was tenuously within reach.

Hundreds of thousands of Chinese soldiers were already on American soil, the first wave having parachuted in to secure the airfields ready for the second wave. The bulk of the follow-up forces landed by ship and spread across the country to their designated positions.

More were arriving every day as the transport planes continued to ferry the remaining troops from the staging areas of Cuba and Venezuela. The second, huge wave of thousands more troops and their associated equipment was currently steaming across the Pacific in the bulk of the Chinese Navy's remaining ships, awaiting final orders as to where to land.

Hundreds of thousands of troops had landed and hundreds of thousands more were arriving imminently, but still Liu criticized the plans.

Against any other country the plan would work by sheer weight of numbers alone. The United States had suffered horrifically from the twelve nuclear detonations over major population centers and strategic targets.

Millions had died instantly in the explosions and blast waves, and millions more were condemned to a slow lingering death caused by radiation poisoning.

The United States, though, had a population of over three hundred and twenty million. It was hurt and hurt badly, but the vastness of the country meant that some entire states had only seen small detachments of Chinese soldiers.

Those giants, containing millions of citizens from one of the most heavily armed countries in the world, could have been kept as sleeping giants—controlled, or at the very least mollified, by carefully controlled media broadcasts and a complete blackout of any others news coming in.

Liu knew that was not the case.

Fen Shu had naively planned that the whole American population would be so cowed and grateful at their arrival that they could soon subjugate and control, using a variety of methods, the whole population.

Her experience, though, came from controlling the uncountable millions of peasants who made up the bulk of the Chinese workforce. For hundreds, if not thousands of years and long before the Communists took control of the vast nation, the Chinese peasants had been controlled and dominated by successive emperors and warlords. Free will and freethinking had been virtually erased from their genetic makeup and any expression of it was immediately erased with maximum force and aggression.

America, however, was built on different foundations. Its strength came from its people. A people who not many generations before had carved, tamed, and created the country using their will power, endurance, and strength. Yes, they had laws and regulations to follow, but freedom was at the heart of the ethos most of them lived by.

Liu knew that if they realized the freedom they cherished so greatly was being taken away from them before the Chinese Army could consolidate its hold over the entire country and its strategic assets, they would be in trouble. The spark of rebellion would turn into a flame and that flame would start a wildfire that would be unstoppable.

Liu then found out that the illness that had started in the camps and spread through the local population was a biological weapon released by Fen Shu. Blankets laced with a virus had been handed out at all the aid stations set up as part of their supposed relief effort. This was her brilliant plan to persuade the captured president of the United States to surrender the country to the invaders with the promise of releasing the cure.

It was also intended to control more of the population. *If they are sick, they cannot fight you*, was the reasoning. And when the cure was released they would be too grateful to remember who it was in the first place who released the virus.

He knew that millions more would die, and her reasoning was completely flawed.

He personally had undertaken in-depth research to understand the minds of one his country's greatest enemies and understood what needed to be done.

Fen Shu hadn't, and in her arrogance had destined the whole mission, in his opinion, to potentially fail.

His mind was racing so much he ran into the back of his savior when he stopped at a door.

"Wait here," hissed the sergeant as he went through the door and closed it behind him.

Liu, blinking in the bright light that flooded through the

briefly opened door, waited, shivering in his bare feet and thin shirt.

The door opened, and his former aide bustled through holding a bag in his hands. "Put these on please, sir," he said politely

Liu looked at him briefly, his face asking the question.

"It is your uniform, sir. You may have lost one when you were arrested, but I retrieved another from your quarters."

He held up the jacket, resplendent with rows of medals and ribbons.

"Quickly please, sir, we must get you out of the city."

Liu stood for a moment and stared at his savior. He was receiving orders from a subordinate. Not twenty-four hours before, whoever had the audacity and stupidity to do such a thing, no matter how correct he or she was, would have been punished severely.

Now he obeyed. Realizing as he did so, struggling with the buttons, that this was the first time in many years he had not dressed without the help of a valet.

His persona changed as he fastened the last button. Removing his uniform and the identity that went with it was an age-old tactic used to control the one you wanted to assume power over.

Now he had his identity back. He was once more a general in the army of the People's Republic of China.

The marine sergeant noticed his change in poise. "Yes, sir.

That's more like it. We are relying on you to get us through all the roadblocks and out of the city before it's too late."

He nodded, assuming that by 'too late,' he meant his escape had been noticed. The sergeant knew otherwise, but now was not the time to tell him what was about to happen.

Exiting the hotel, he was surprised to see his official car with his nation's flag attached to the hood fluttering in the wind that whipped through the narrow alleyway.

In minutes he was speeding through the city. No soldier at any roadblock or checkpoint had the nerve to even think of stopping the progress of the VIP obscured from view behind the deeply tinted windows of the official-looking car.

CHAPTER
THREE

SOMEWHERE ON THE I-64, VIRGINIA

Cal and the twenty-four other passengers stood staring at the sky. Only moments before they had been on the bus that was conveying them to a ship due to repatriate them back to their own countries and away from the war zone they had unexpectedly found themselves in.

From different European countries, as was the usual, the shared common language was English, which they all spoke with greater or lesser degrees of fluency.

This suited Cal fine, as his, along with most of the British population's foreign language skills, had not developed beyond being able to order a drink at a bar in whatever your European holiday destination was that year.

Most of his fellow passengers did not know what the high-up chemtrails meant. He did. He was also party to other information that he knew his travelling companions were in ignorance of.

The chatter between them began. Cal needed to stop it before wild speculation and hysteria caused the panic and poor decisions that would follow.

Not one to want to stand out from the crowd, he was usually happy for others to take the lead on things. His confidence since leaving the Royal Marines had slowly been sucked away as his relationship with Angie (even though he'd persuaded himself it was what he wanted) blossomed and followed the traditional path. They dated for a while, then they moved in together, then came the marriage plans only for him to be dumped just weeks before the big event when she ran off with his supposed best mate.

A broken man, he stubbornly went on the honeymoon alone. It was all paid for anyway and with no possibility of a refund he did not want to give the woman he had considered the love of his life the tickets, so she could enjoy what he had spent his lifesavings and more on with the person who was going to be the best man at their wedding.

His life changed in more ways than one in New York. He had wandered the city full of loneliness, anger, and despair, taking faked happy selfies at all the usual landmarks, posting them on social media to prove to the world he was doing fine.

Then he met Louise. A beautiful West Virginian whose only aim in life was to live it. As soon as she had enough money saved from working as a waitress in her hometown, she was off to wherever her wanderlust took her.

One drink-fuelled night of craziness bought them together. Never having met anyone like her before his feelings for her grew every hour they spent together.

Thrown even closer together following the terror attacks in New York that heralded the start of Chinese aggression, they escaped the city along with others only to fall ill to radiation poisoning. He nursed her for days, himself desperately ill until he fulfilled her dying wish to return to her own home.

It was fulfilling that wish that bought him in contact with the resistance. They wanted his help.

Initially cautious and unsure, it took Louise's death to make him join them. He had found someone to love again and she had been wrenched from his grasp before he could tell her.

He wanted to avenge her death.

Silently girding his loins, he prepared himself, pushing his self-doubt aside and building up his inner confidence. These people needed his help and he alone could do it. He could lead them to a safer place.

He walked into the middle of the group and called for quiet. "Hi, my name is Cal and I, like you, was being sent home after being released from a camp, much like yourselves I imagine."

Heads nodded as they listened.

"What you do not know is that I was sent to a camp by the resistance to send information out to help them in planning an attack to liberate it."

Immediately he was besieged with questions, but he held up his hands and called for quiet again.

"Please let me finish and then you can ask as many questions as you like. The last message I received was to expect the attack at two o'clock today."

He pointed up at the sky. "I do not know if they are part of the attack, but it's about that time now so my best guess is that whatever was planned was not just local, but part of a greater co-ordinated strike. The soldiers guarding us on the bus had some sort of warning over their radios and probably seeing what was overhead, panicked and deserted us. I have a few suggestions as to what we do next, but I would say if this is the beginning of the fight back, then we best avoid any areas where the Chinese are concentrated."

A young pretty brunette spoke up. She spoke English, but with a heavy French accent. "Why? We need to reach the ship that will take us away from this."

Others nodded in agreement around her.

Cal pointed to the sky again. Still more chemtrails were following the others, their altitude making their progress seem slow whereas in reality they were streaking though the atmosphere at hundreds of miles an hour.

"Do you know what they are?" He didn't wait for an answer. "They are cruise missiles. I do not know which country fired them, but they could contain either a high explosive or a nuclear warhead. The Chinese have already made this conflict nuclear so do not even begin to imagine others won't baulk from using them.

"We were all being taken to Norfolk to board this ship that was taking us home. If I remember correctly Norfolk is a major US naval base. The base must therefore be under Chinese control. That will most likely make it a target for one of those things up there. I for one am not prepared to take that risk. The safest place for us to be right now is as far away from any Chinese as we can."

Another person spoke up. "We are not Americans, it is not our war. Our countries must get us home."

A man stepped forward, his privileged-filled home-counties accent matched the now bedraggled business suit he was wearing. "Cal, I believe you are right. Our passports will offer us no protection now. If the Chinese bastards are being attacked, then anyone who doesn't look like them will now become their enemy."

He turned and pointed toward Cal. "I think we should listen to what this young man has to say. He has had contact with the American resistance and if what he has just told us is correct then they, I imagine, are in contact with whoever is responsible for what is flying over us now. Our route home now lies with them and not the Chinese."

His plummy cultured accent carried a natural authority to it.

More heads were now nodding in agreement and eyes were turning to Cal.

Cal nodded his thanks to the man. He stood silent for a while, contemplating what they should do next.

"The keys are still in the bus. If we can find a map, then we can start planning a route. I'll need everyone's help with this. We have come from different camps and areas. If we could mark on where people know there are troops, we can try to work a route around them."

Most of the passengers agreed to join them. Four though, a French couple and two Spanish women, could not be swayed and they set off walking still adamant their best option lay at the coast. Cal watched them leave, knowing they were making a mistake that could cost them their lives.

After a quick survey, Cal was the only one who had any experience driving large vehicles due to his work in construction. He sat in the driver's seat, and after a few crunches of gears, turned the bus around and they set off.

CHAPTER
FOUR

RUSSIAN GOVERNMENT WAR BUNKER

President Petrov sat at the head of the large table positioned in the middle of the cavernous room. Filling the rest of the table was the entire cabinet and representatives from all branches of the military. The walls around him were covered with large screens showing everything from satellite imagery to Western news channels. Banks of computers and communications equipment lined the walls below them, attended to by a legion of uniformed soldiers, all studiously and silently working away. Occasional glances were cast at their great leader sat a mere few yards away.

The bunker was one of many built during the Soviet regime around the periphery of Moscow. They were far enough away to avoid the effects of a direct hit by a high-yield nuclear weapon on Moscow, but close enough that they could easily be reached in times of crisis. Petrov favored this one. Its stark raw concrete construction didn't hide behind any trappings of luxury as other bunkers that had been built for the elite were. He wanted to feel that if the country was at war and suffering then why should those leading them experience any sort of luxury. The vast complex could accommodate hundreds of people comfortably but not *in* comfort. He smiled as he heard a few mutterings of complaint about the starkness of their quarters whilst he was waiting for one of his generals to arrive and report the progress so far.

Good, he thought to himself, hiding his contempt for those who complained behind a smile. *These fat pigs need to experience this more often, we are Russians and not soft pampered Westerners.*

His musings were interrupted by the arrival of the general and his aides. The president began before the general even had time to sit down. "Welcome, General. Before we discuss America can you please tell the committee members how the domestic situation is proceeding."

"Sir, all is proceeding to plan. The evacuation of the cities has commenced. There have been the usual delays and foul ups, but none that are unexpected and are not of concern.

"The citizens are mainly being cooperative. The camps we are constructing to house them are keeping up with the incoming flow and as more arrive we have more labor available to direct toward the projects.

"The timing of this is, for once, in our favor. The spring weather is mild, and summer is fast approaching. We may have many challenges to deal with, but a winter is one we do not need to consider for a while. The request we broadcast appealing for every citizen to do their duty for the motherland has worked beyond all expectations. Every base is filling with reserve personnel. They are arriving by their thousands every hour and there is no sign of the flood stopping."

The general chuckled. "We are even turning away old soldiers no longer on our lists. I believe the oldest so far is an eighty-five-year-old Korean war veteran, who claims to have fought in the Great Patriotic War as a young boy."

Petrov interrupted him. "If they want to fight, let them. If they have experience, then we can use them. They may not be fit for frontline duty, but they can take the place of one who is. From now on, General, turn no one away."

He looked at his cabinet for confirmation. They all nodded. He chuckled wryly to himself. "And anyway, I am sure our esteemed media department will love such stories. General, please continue."

"We are surging soldiers east along the railway. Old bases mothballed for decades are being reopened. The warehouses storing all the materiel needed to arm them are being opened and their contents distributed.

"Soon we will have millions of soldiers in position ready and willing to protect the motherland. As per orders we are not moving any troops toward the border, but those already stationed there are reporting no enemy activity whatsoever. I ordered a few small patrols to cross the border last night. The men know the area well and continuously play cat and mouse games with their Chinese counterparts.

"They know we do it and we know they do it. The game is to see how far you can get before getting detected. It is not unknown for a 'captive' from either side to be invited into the opposition's mess for a drink before being sent home, once they have been searched for any intelligence that is. The friendliness is unofficially allowed by both sides as it stops the game getting out of hand and the ensuing diplomatic problems it would cause.

"What the patrol found was interesting in its lack of content. They found nothing. Most of the border posts were deserted, and those that were manned were not garrisoned by the usual border guards who receive a good level of training, but by ones who were so inept in their discipline that they may as well not have been there."

Petrov interrupted again. "So, you are telling me that at a time when we are mobilizing millions of troops to help protect our borders, China's frontier is as exposed as it has been at no time before?"

"Yes, sir. China has emptied her cupboards to support the American operation. Strategically, they would commit their best troops to the plan. It is how many we do not know at this stage. We are currently working through the intelligence to give you a more accurate count."

"Do not give me accurate, General! We do not have time for an analyst to agonize over a few thousand here or there. The war will be over by then," Petrov barked. "We have seen what they have done. We know how many ships have landed and how many are still at sea. We know they flew the first waves in from Cuba and Venezuela. I need your best estimate of what we are facing. Accuracy can wait for the history books."

The general, unruffled by the apparent anger of his president, sifted through some papers on the desk in front of him before finding the one he was looking for. "I thought you may ask, sir.

"We estimate there were approximately two hundred thousand frontline elite troops committed to the first wave. The last of these are still arriving by transport planes from both Cuba and Venezuela. More are arriving hourly direct from China now the main airfields are secured. We estimate that almost every commercial airline they have is involved in bringing the next wave in.

"The majority of the Chinese Navy is currently closing on the Western Seaboard of the United States. The net they have thrown around themselves utilizing both surface ships and submarines is very effective and we have not been able to get close yet to report fully."

He held up his hand as he could see Petrov's anger building again. "We estimate over seventy-five percent of their fleet is at sea carrying at least another fifty to seventy-five thousand troops.

If we include the navy and air force personnel involved they have committed over five hundred thousand to the operation. These ships will also most likely be transporting most of their heavy equipment. And those personnel on board will again be their best trained and best armed."

Petrov nodded. "Tell me how the American operation is proceeding so far."

"The Canadians are being very cooperative. They have fully mobilized and have called up all reserves for duty. They have opened up all of their bases for us and we are coordinating with them currently how best to proceed.

"The two Air Assault Brigades we deployed immediately to Canada last night parachuted into San Antonio, Texas to find and release the President of the United States."

Petrov knew this, but he let him continue for the sake of the rest around the table. "Following information from agents in place we received confirmation of her location and that she was about to sign the surrender of the United States of America to China. That as we know cannot be allowed to happen because it would immediately legitimize everything they had set out to achieve. Rescuing her from captivity is of the utmost priority."

An aged colonel general sitting at the lower end of the table spoke up. "Two brigades. Will that be enough to take a city?"

The general looked at his colleague; he knew he had served his whole life in the military, his unwavering loyalty to the state enabling him to survive the political upheavals of the past decades. He carried many scars from putting himself too close to the action at many stages of his career before being offered the General Officer role where his advice and council was always listened to and treated with respect.

"No, Colonel General. Not nearly enough. But it was all we had to put into theatre at short notice. The information came through the resistance movement who we are coordinating our efforts with.

"Without them the mission could not have happened. My men have parachuted into an unknown city against an unknown number of enemy soldiers with no more intelligence than laminated copies of street maps printed off the Internet. The local militias have mobilized and have already started a guerrilla warfare campaign led by a former CIA agent. They have infiltrated the city ready to link up with our forces once the target is located and secured.

"At the same time the air assault began we, together with the American Navy, launched a cruise missile strike against known Chinese concentrations of forces as a diversion.

"Over two hundred missiles with conventional warheads have been launched, more could have been launched but resupply is an issue. It was thought best to evaluate the success of the strikes and to husband available resources."

The minister of health interrupted him. "Why were we not

consulted? I came to this meeting to find that not only have we invaded a foreign soil, but we have launched hundreds of missiles."

In the silence that followed, the minister squirmed uncomfortably under Petrov's scrutiny.

"You are quite right, Minister. But time was short, and decisions needed to be made whilst you were sleeping in your quarters."

Petrov leaned forward staring straight into the minister's eyes. "Tell me, comrade. Would you have voted against such action? If your answer is yes, I would be interested in understanding why. If your vote would have been for it, then why are you complaining? Or is it the actions of a man sulking, his pride being hurt that the world keeps turning without him? Tell me how you would have voted."

The minister, a new appointee, regretted opening his mouth in a badly thought-out attempt to make an impression on the room, and tried to extricate himself from the situation. He stumbled through an apology, saying of course the president was right in what he did.

Petrov, though, did not let it go. "Thank you, Minister, for your vote of confidence. Now as the general explained earlier, millions of our loyal citizens need our help. They have been displaced from their homes and are now living in hastily built camps. As minister for health I need a report from you about how your department is helping them and what more we can do for them. I am relying on you to do this for your country. I suggest you organize an immediate personal visit to these camps to best understand what is required of you. Please do not let me stop you. You can leave now to start on this crucial project and I look forward to receiving your report in due course."

Dismissed and outmaneuvered, the man could do no more than collect his papers from the desk and, trying to regain his dignity, walk briskly from the room. Petrov looked around the rest of the room. The message was clear. You were with him or against him and there was no room around the table for the latter.

The colonel general, too old to care about who he upset, knew the mood in the room needed to change. He grumbled softly, his voice deepened by the forty cigarettes he still smoked daily. "Before we were so rudely interrupted can I just check the facts because I think otherwise I might be going senile at last. We have invaded America with their permission after staging through Canada to help fight a Chinese occupying force who have nuked half of the country. Comrade, President, you got me. Great joke. Now can we get to the main news of the day and talk about who is going to win the World Cup."

The laughter by everyone including Petrov dispersed any tension that remained in the room.

CHAPTER
FIVE

SAN ANTONIO, TEXAS

Colonel Wong, a colonel in the Chinese Army, after the arrest of General Liu the day before, worried what his own future would hold. He had respected and admired his general, agreeing with his criticism of how the campaign had been waged and the decisions made by people with no military or tactical knowledge. He knew the charges against him were wholly made up and had no credence. His greatest fear was that as an ally of General Liu, he may be tarnished with the same brush and face similar accusations if he did not please his political masters.

In the absence of Liu, he was ordered to continue to make sure the city was safe for the visiting dignitaries who had arrived for the surrender ceremony. The spate of bombings and unrest that were becoming a daily occurrence in some places must not be allowed to happen on such an important day. Given little time to organize he used all his skill to formulate a plan. Extra troops were called in from outlying areas to bolster the already strong city-based force.

Concentrating most of the force in and around the area the ceremony was going to take place, he also placed large numbers of troops nearby in strategic places to act as a quick reaction force. All citizens were evacuated from the area and he put strict movement controls in place. In the short time he was given he was satisfied he had done a professional and comprehensive job.

He was in a mobile control center set up close to the ceremony location when the missiles started to fall from the sky. The distant *crump* of high explosives told him something was wrong seconds before the calls started coming in over the comms.

Before he could piece together the information, bursts of automatic gunfire close by told his instincts he probably had more urgent and closer problems to deal with.

Stepping out of the mobile trailer he looked around in shock. Some soldiers guarding his unit were firing at paratroopers descending from the sky in large numbers, whilst the others were engaging some who had already landed. Rushing inside he grabbed a set of binoculars off a table and went back outside.

It took him a few seconds to focus in on one of the descending bodies spiraling down as they tried to avoid the incoming fire. One look told him all he needed to know. "Fucking Russians," he cursed as he dove back into the trailer, adding a long and offensive vitriol in his native Mandarin.

His only objective was not his personal safety, but to get orders out to his area commanders to mobilize every unit he had to counter the threat. He spent a few seconds studying the large-scale map on the wall enabling him to formulate the orders. If he had known that those few seconds were all the time he had left in the world he would have spent them screaming orders down the radio.

***

Corporal Sergei Ramius was one of the first on the ground. Since landing only moments before, he and his comrades had been pinned down by an unexpectedly large concentration of enemy soldiers pouring accurate and sustained fire in their direction. Returning fire, he noticed the corner of a large mobile unit with multiple aerials protruding from the roof poking out from the corner of a building.

He shouted across to his sergeant who was firing from behind the cover of a large tree.

"Dmitri. There is a command trailer just around the corner. If you keep the bastard's heads down I can get into a better position to take the shot."

Sergei was their unit's demolitions specialist. He carried, strapped across his back, an RPG-7D3, the version of the infamous weapon that was designed for airborne troops to utilize in the field. His relationship with the weapon bordered on the romantic and he lived for the times he could fire it.

The sergeant acknowledged his understanding with a wave and bawled for the men within his hearing range to increase their rate of fire.

The corporal took full advantage as the Chinese sheltered from the withering volume the paratroopers lay down. Crawling from cover to cover he cautiously peered around the car he was behind to check his position. He now had a good angle to take a shot at the trailer.

Normally operating in two-man units, he had not seen his loader since the jump. He did not know it, but he had been killed in the descent by a well-aimed shot from a Chinese soldier. Unslinging the launcher and rucksack of additional warheads from his back, he assembled the rocket by screwing in the propellant charge to the warhead. Carefully but quickly he inserted the rocket into the launcher, making sure it was located correctly, and finally removed the safety cap on the fuse. The weapon was ready to fire.

Risking another glance, he quickly worked out the trailer was roughly fifty meters away. An easy shot for most with an RPG, but Sergei was an expert capable of hitting targets far beyond the effective range of the weapon. Rising from cover with the weapon mounted on his shoulder and ready to fire all he needed was a moment to acquire the target and pull the trigger.

As soon as he pulled the trigger he dropped back behind cover. He did not need to see if he had hit the target as he already knew he had. The rocket covered the distance in less than half a second.

***

Colonel Wong picked up the handset to send out the orders that would flood the city with soldiers. Just as he depressed the transmit button the rocket pierced the side of the trailer and exploded, killing him and everyone inside instantly.

Such is the hand of fate on a battlefield; if he had sent out the orders the Russian paratroopers would not have stood a chance and would have soon been overwhelmed, and Madeline Tanner would have been back in Chinese custody. As it was, no orders were sent to the commanders of the thousands of troops stationed all around the city, and they waited, listening to the sounds of battle raging a mere few miles away, but not daring to advance without orders. Thousands of Chinese soldiers, though, were already in the city, fighting the enemy that had dropped from the sky. They were fighting in units, advancing toward the nearest enemy soldiers. When the command trailer was destroyed, so was the ability to coordinate them into one cohesive force.

****

Fen Shu was in a complete panic.

Today was supposed to be her crowning glory. One that would send her career up to the stratosphere. She was going to be the person who delivered the United States of America, wrapped up and bundled in an official declaration of surrender to the People's Republic of China.

After this her power would increase to unimaginable levels. The misogynistic party leadership could no longer sneer at a mere woman daring to impose herself on a man's world. She recognized that those who knew that she was the niece of the president thought she was only in her position because of him, and in a way, they were correct. It was to prove those old men who ruled the country with unlimited powers wrong why she drove herself and her ambitions forward continually. Hatching the plan to steal America and then using all her guile and skills to get the plan approved at the highest levels had taken her years of careful manipulating and maneuvering.

China didn't need to conquer the United States. Over the last few decades it virtually had without a shot being fired. Through unfair trade practices and downright cheating and stealing it had built up its industrial and manufacturing base: using its unlimited and very cheap labor force to work in the factories, producing goods far cheaper than anyone else could; ignoring every safety and environmental concern. They eventually dominated the world's economy. The money that poured into the country was turned around and used to buy up assets and debt in all corners of the globe, until every government in the developed world was beholden to them.

The United States of America was and always had been the thorn in their side. A true global superpower. Only they had the power and influence to challenge them in their desire to be the biggest and most powerful country on earth. It was like two bullies challenging each other in the playground with the weaker one never having the nerve to pick a fight they knew they couldn't win. But this bully had hatched a plan to hurt its opponent and then attack when it was temporarily weakened.

Dragging Madeline Tanner by the arm, she, along with her personal guard, had rushed into a coffee shop as the unknown soldiers landed by parachute on the street outside. Moments before her phone had rung telling her unknown aircraft were approaching and missiles were falling from the sky, raining death and destruction wherever they hit. She still had the arrogance to not understand why anyone would have the audacity to attack them. Did they not know who they were dealing with?

The fact that her plan had already caused millions of innocent people to die in the nuclear holocaust—not including those millions more who would die horribly, poisoned by the fallout—did not occur to her. Whoever was attacking them had no right to do so and she would ensure they were punished.

Her security detail thought differently.

They were loyal Chinese citizens, trusted with protecting the leaders of their nation. To get to such a position their loyalty would no doubt have been rigorously tested to the highest degree. Many tried, but only the best of the best made it.

They feared Fen Shu but, to a man, they did not respect her. Having secured the coffee shop they had sought shelter in, they tried in vain to call for backup over their radios.

The channel reserved for security officials for the higher ranks was full of others calling for assistance. Trying other channels, the story was the same. Every unit was either engaged with the enemy that had fallen from the skies or was requesting orders.

Looking out the window made any thought of surrender vanish. They watched as an isolated squad of Chinese soldiers, caught out on the open, bravely tried to fight back. The trained eyes of the bodyguards could see the men were in a hopeless position, outnumbered and caught in an indefensible position by what could only be elite forces. They were picked off easily. The last three alive, with no other option left, surrendered.

They did so without shame, they had fought bravely against insurmountable odds until the only choices left were death or surrender. Dropping their weapons and with hands raised they walked from what little cover they had utilized.

The opposing soldiers broke cover too and approached them. Keeping tight squad formation, with the rest holding their weapons ready, still scanning for threats from all quadrants, two of the soldiers approached them giving the universal hand signals to get on the floor. As soon as they complied they raised their weapons and fired short controlled bursts at the prone soldiers, riddling them with bullets and killing them instantly. The bodyguards looked at each other. They would do their utmost to save Fen Shu, because in doing so they could save their own lives.

Fen Shu knew she had to get away. She was still holding the biggest bargaining chip they possessed by the arm. Madeline Tanner had recovered from the shock at the unexpected turn of events. Soldiers had parachuted in and were killing the Chinese. She was in no doubt, they had to be American and they were here to save her.

She looked at Fen Shu and yanked her arm free from her grip. "You bitch!" she screamed at her.

Her shame and humiliation at being captured so easily, and the way she had been treated since, transformed into the rage that had been building up inside her. This woman had tried to manipulate her, and she had played along. She had been forced into surrendering her country because she wanted to help it. Its people needed the cure for the virus that Fen Shu had callously unleashed, and the price of that cure was the country. But she knew she was not the country. No God-fearing American would accept being ruled by a foreign power and she knew the surrender would not end it. They would fight back.

Now she was going to fight back. Screaming swear words that would make a sailor blush she drew back her arm, bunched her fist and released all her anger into a punch that would have made a prizefighter proud.

Fen's head snapped back, and her nose exploded. The force of the punch propelled her light body across the tiled floor of the shop ending up in an unconscious heap against the serving counter. The guards turned and stared in shock at the sight of their principal sprawled unconscious on the floor. Madeline, toughened from years of verbal fighting as a politician, had also not got where she was without perfecting the ability to read people. The men in front of her, although armed and far stronger than her, were scared.

And scared people always looked for a way out.

She stood staring at the men crouching behind the low wall they had sought shelter behind that divided the shop. "It's over, you have lost. Drop your weapons and get out."

She knew they understood her; they had given her commands in English when they had kept watch on her before. Madeline could see them wavering with indecision. She changed her tactic smoothly.

She lowered her voice to a softer, more reasoning level. "You are not in uniform. If you lose your weapons and get out of here, you can hide. As soon as they have me I am sure they will withdraw. Don't get yourselves killed over some stupid sense of loyalty. It's over, at least try to save yourselves." She looked and pointed theatrically out of the window. "They will be here soon. Go now, while you can."

The four men looked at each other. The lead agent stood up and faced Madeline. "We are sorry for the nuclear attacks," one of them said apologetically, "that was not the honorable way to start this war. Please accept our apologies." He issued a curt command in Mandarin to the others and they quickly obeyed, removing their side arms and laying the compact submachine guns they ordinarily carried concealed under their coats on a table. Without a word they filed through to the back of the shop. Madeline heard a door open and close and then she was alone. Alone apart from Agent Fen Shu who was starting to move as she came around from the knockout punch. Acting quickly Madeline picked up one of the handguns, checked it was safe, and slung one of the machine guns over her shoulder.

She was familiar with firearms. Her husband, Steve, was a keen hunter. Though not a regular shooter, she had enough experience to know which end was the dangerous one and how not to hurt yourself or others when handling one. By the time Fen Shu was fully conscious, Madeline had used a power cord to bind her hands behind her back and her feet together. The first thing she saw when her eyes came into focus was her former prisoner crouching down next to her pointing a gun at her face.

"Let me go. You will pay for this insolence. You American whore."

Madeline shoved the pistol into her mouth breaking two of her expensively maintained teeth off at the roots in the process. "Call me whore again, sweetie," she said with an evil smile, "and I will start shooting your fingers off."

The sounds of firing still echoed around the offices and high-rises of the city. "Do you hear that? That is the sound of your failure. You may have won the first round, but did you think America was going to roll over and just give up? We are not a country full of peasants you can control by force. If that was the case the United States would have disappeared into history long ago. I was going to surrender the country to you to try and get the medical attention the people desperately needed. I was doing it for humanitarian reasons and not out of weakness. You just don't understand why I would do that, do you?"

Fen Shu screamed at her, her voice distorted by the broken teeth and blood pouring from her mouth and nose. "I will never surrender to you. You will have to kill me first."

Madeline laughed in her face. Something Fen Shu had not had happen to her since she was an orphan begging on the streets. She flashed back to that time long ago. The world was simple, all her and her brother needed to do was to get enough food to eat each day. It all changed suddenly when her brother was hit by a car and their situation was discovered. With no thought for sibling love the two were separated. Fen Shu never saw her brother again, despite using all the connections and influence she gained in later life after being adopted by a wealthy family.

The only slim lead she ever had was that the orphanage her brother disappeared from was known to sell children to foreigners. It was illegal but tolerated by the authorities. One less child to look after saved them money after all, and if a rich foreigner wanted to pay good money for one, then more fool them.

She discovered that most of the children were sold to child-less American couples desperate at any cost to have the chance to raise a child they could call their own. No records were ever kept and when staff at the orphanage were questioned no one remembered a single young boy from all the thousands they dealt with.

Her only revenge was to have the manager, who was still in charge of the orphanage at that time, arrested and executed on trumped-up treason charges.

No psychiatrist had ever treated Fen Shu. To even think of seeing one was a sign of weakness that if discovered would destroy your career. If she had been treated, her pathological hatred and need to destroy America could have been resolved in therapy. Fen Shu's eyes flickered as the memory of her brother raced through her brain. She always hoped she would find him, she promised herself she would and now the reality hit her. She had not only failed in her mission to conquer America, she had failed on the promise she had made to herself to find her brother.

She was suddenly unsure as to what failure hurt more.

Madeline looked up, soldiers were approaching the coffee shop. A quick look showed they were not Chinese. She tucked the pistol into the waistband of her skirt and slowly approached the glass, her hands held out to show she was not holding a weapon.

The soldiers saw her though the window and weapons were raised in her direction.

Madeline looked at the soldiers in confusion. In her many years as a politician she had seen all sorts of military uniforms worn by all branches of the services, but these soldiers were wearing a uniform she didn't recognize, and their weapons were different too. They had the distinctive curved magazine favored by Soviet troops. She knew enough that most had moved on from the ubiquitous AK-47 and they were called something else now, but she couldn't remember.

She paused, unsure what to do next. Two soldiers, still with their weapons pointed at her, entered the shop.

"Hello. I'm Madeline Tanner, President of the United States of America. I think you may be looking for me." One of the soldiers pulled a picture from a pocket on his trousers and compared the image to her. He broke into a grin and saluted speaking in heavily accented broken English. His voice sounded to her like a movie villain from the eighties.

"Sergeant Michael Levinko, at your service Madam President. People vill be very happy to see you."

He turned and spoke rapidly to his men and then into his radio, looking at a map and, with his tongue getting caught on the unfamiliar street names, he repeated their current location. Within minutes, more soldiers began appearing, coming from all directions as they ran to their location. Under direction of others they began to spread out in an outward-facing cordon centered around her location.

The sergeant turned to her. "We wait here. Rescue will be coming soon."

Chapter Six

Staff Sergeant Eddie Edmunds was tired to the bone. Since the 'uprising,' as the locals proudly began calling their efforts to release themselves from the yolk of Chinese rule, he and the community had been working tirelessly to secure their position, expecting at any moment for an unstoppable Chinese retaliation to arrive in the form of heavy armor and high explosives.

Only a few had been party to the plan they'd hatched using the weekly pierogi-making meetings as cover. Operational security was key to the success of any mission. The Chinese had arrived in such force on an unprepared population still reeling from the news of the nuclear attacks that the humanitarian story they spun was initially believable. The lie was soon seen through as, although ordinary citizens were left alone, any law enforcement or military personnel either active or reserve were sought out and targeted.

Some escaped, some were captured, but most resisted, their futile attempts met with a one-sided hail of lead. Leaders emerged and not from the places you would expect them to come from. Housewives, local farmers, and businessmen quietly stepped up to the plate and began discreetly making plans.

Eddie, a Marine Staff Sergeant, had been on leave from his training role at Camp Pendleton, south of Los Angeles. He tried to get back to see his folks as often as his duties allowed, taking advantage of at last being posted in the same state, and made the long road trip home at every opportunity.

His parents were elderly now. They'd adopted him later in life after realizing they could not have children naturally, but still wanted to raise a child they could call their own.

Both being Caucasian and being considered too old to adopt under the local rules, they did as many other couples chose to do and adopted a child from China. There were many agencies that offered, in exchange for money to smooth out the red tape, the chance to adopt an orphan who otherwise would have a bleak future in a country that held little regard for the welfare of the unfortunate. He had a happy childhood. His parents loved him and gave him every opportunity and chance that their modest lives allowed. Conscious of his Chinese heritage and not wanting him to forget where he came from, they encouraged him to be proud of his background. They ensured he attended Mandarin classes and other groups set up by parents in similar situations where adopted

Chinese children had the chance to meet.

When the nuclear bombs exploded, and the invasion happened, his first thought was to immediately report back to his base. The last thing he saw though before the television channels shut down was a report of all the bases that had been destroyed in the nuclear blasts and the heavy conventional bombings that followed.

Camp Pendleton was on that list.

The arrival of the first Chinese soldiers and the immediate travel ban imposed, purportedly for their own safety, forced him to stay in Swall. Having not lived in the valley for many years, and so not appearing on any census or residential lists, he had managed to avoid the roundups of known servicemen and women. He watched through trained eyes as they smoothly and quickly took over control. He knew he had to do something to help free his country from the foreign invaders. He knew he was Chinese and outwardly looked no different to the thousands of armed men and women who arrived uninvited and unwanted. Even though he was of Chinese origin, he felt he was no more Chinese than an alien from outer space was. He was American, and it was his duty both as a citizen and a serving soldier of his country to fight for its freedom.

How he looked had all the way through his life stood him apart from others. During his formative years he withstood the occasional racist comments and subtle jibes that were said to his face or behind his back. His parents, understanding this would happen, prepared him and gave him the mental toughness to ignore it.

Even though he didn't realize it himself, it never got him down. It had the opposite effect, in fact. He made himself be the most American person he could. Surely no 'Slitty-eyed Commie Chink' would still hold the school's season touchdown record or score the winning goal in the county basketball championship. One also definitely would not be asked by Megan Jones, the head cheerleader and most beautiful girl in school, to be her date to the school prom. But he did.

For once his looks could work to his and everyone's advantage

Getting a uniform was easy. The local launderette was commandeered by the Chinese and local women were ordered to work there. A few missing uniforms from all the hundreds washed everyday would not be noticed. After donning the uniform, he stole an unfortunate soldier's sloppily unattended weapon and webbing and blended in with the invaders.

It was at the pierogi club that he was pretending to guard where he had first met others and the plan was hatched to poison Fat Joe's tomatoes which they knew were being distributed to feed the soldiers. The outwardly willing locals set to work, gaining positions of trust with the Chinese. The ricin was manufactured easily. The local school's chemistry teacher gathered and processed caster beans from the many plants of that name that grew wildly in the area.

The workers sent to Fat Joe's farm had been carefully selected and told what to do with the small packets of highly toxic powder. Unaware of the doses required the tomatoes were poisoned with far more than was needed. This helped, though, as if only traces of the toxin were present the process, even though the end result would be the same, would take longer. The soldiers ingesting the massive doses were all dead by Sunday morning.

The few that escaped the poisoning were hunted down and killed by packs of locals, desperate to avenge loved ones and friends that had been killed directly by the Chinese or by the killer virus that had struck down a large portion of the population. Eddie stood outside the town hall which was being used to collect and sort through the huge quantity of weapons gathered from the dead soldiers.

The community had all mobilized. The dead were cleared away and buried in mass graves. The few locals who had escaped the purges and had military experience were given the job of preparing to defend the area. Eddie became their de facto leader. Their small but significant victory had killed hundreds of their enemy, but they knew there were hundreds of thousands more in the country and more on the way.

If discovered, which would only be a matter of time, they would expect no quarter to be given. They had crossed the line and must get ready to defend the freedom they had just earned with their lives.

Standing in the sun outside the town hall he watched a young girl happily playing in the park across the street, watched over by her mother. Her laughter struck a chord of a long ago, deeply buried memory.

He remembered his younger sister, but the memory was from such a different and distant part of his life that he rarely thought of her. When he had settled in America and his confidence and language had developed enough, he remembered distinctly the night he told his adoptive parents he had left a sister behind in China.

They were horrified and extremely upset to have been responsible for splitting them up. The adoption agency had given them no more background on him other than he was found living on the streets after being orphaned when both his parents were killed. There was no mention of a sister at all, otherwise they told him they would have adopted both of them.

His parents did try. They contacted the agency he had been adopted through and even employed a private detective in China to investigate, but no news about his sister was ever found. It was as if she had never existed. The girl's laughter reminded him of his long-lost sister. He wondered if she was alive and what had become of her.

CHAPTER SEVEN

Cal drove the bus onwards into the evening. Acting as his navigator was the older Englishman Gordon, who had helped persuade the international group of refugees that their best hope lay in following Cal to try and find the resistance fighters he had already met. His finger plotted their course on the only map they had been able to find, a small-scale map covering half of the Eastern seaboard of the United States.

The map the Chinese soldiers had abandoned on the bus was of no use to them. It had been manufactured for them specifically and was covered in unintelligible logograms and made no sense to any of them. Combining the group's scant knowledge of what they had experienced they drew up the best route to follow. It was working and the bus, slowly chugging along, was taking them ever so slowly and cautiously to the cross Cal had marked on the map.

The roads when the bombing and invasion started were at first chaotic as everyone who could, fled. Following the initial panic, the road traffic had dropped to be virtually non-existent. Those who wanted to be somewhere else had tried, but in most cases failed, to get there, as they encountered the strategically set up roadblocks positioned by the Chinese to do exactly as they planned, which was to cripple the country's transportation network.

Most of these people ended up in the camps and were now among the millions suffering from the biological weapon released on the tainted blankets they slept under. The rest hunkered down in their homes, waiting. Or if they had the skill and knowledge, had packed up and headed to the hills where many joined together, creating sprawling backwoods campsites far away from roads and towns. Stretching out dwindling supplies, hoping for news.

Gordon looked up from the map. "I am not quite sure where we are, but those are the Appalachians we can see rising ahead. If my memory serves me correctly they should be even more sparsely populated than we are finding it now. It may be a good idea to find somewhere to stop for the night. We are all just about done in and driving off the edge of a mountain road is not going to do any of us any good."

Cal looked at him, a smile creeping across his tired face. "The Appalachians? Surely, and according to Laurel and Hardy, the mountains in Virginia are the Blue Ridge ones."

Gordon chuckled at Cal's attempt at humor. "Yes, they are, and you are correct. But for the sake of a geography lesson I will not educate you otherwise."

He pointed ahead out of the window; the road was already rising forcing Cal to change down through the gears as they entered the foothills.

"Cal, take us to the Blue Ridge Mountains. But if you ask me to find you a lonesome pine, you can bloody well find it yourself!" The brief moment of levity passed when Cal looked down at the fuel gauge. It was hovering above the red line.

"We need to find some fuel for this thing soon otherwise we are going to be riding Shanks's pony and I don't fancy yomping the rest of the way." Cal was still in poor shape, recovering from the grief of losing Louise and the radiation poisoning that had almost killed him. His hair had stopped falling out but the bare patches covering his head probably made the way he was feeling look worse.

"Yomping. Now that's an expression that takes me back. Tell me Cal, have you served at some point?"

"I was a Royal Marine. Did a few tours in Afghanistan before I had seen enough and got out. I have been working in construction ever since."

"Ah, which brigade?"

"Four-two."

Gordon dropped the map and looked at him. "My word! You are not going to believe this. So was I."

Cal almost steered the bus off the road. He braked and brought the bus to a stop and stared at Gordon. "No way!"

Gordon saluted saying, "Lieutenant Gordon Scott, Four-Two Commando at your service. Saw a bit of action in the Falklands before I too decided to try life on Civvy Street."

Cal automatically returned the Salute. "Lance Corporal Owen Calhoun, Four-Two Commando, at yours too. Yomping! I can never complain about that because you did the mother of all yomps back then." They shook hands happily and vigorously. Cal was referring to the incident which made the expression famous. During the Falklands Conflict in 1982, with their transport sunk, the Royal Marines completed a grueling fifty-six-mile, three-day 'yomp' over terrible terrain to take the fight to the Argentinian forces. The photo of a marine with a Union flag attached to his radio mast became one of the iconic pictures of the war. Knowing exactly what he was referring to Gordon smiled and shook his head.

"Ah I wasn't involved in that particular event. That was four-zero. But I did walk a fair way myself across that desolate turd of a place. Those buggers after that thought they were all film stars and never let us forget it." The other passengers on the bus, wondering why they had suddenly stopped, were beginning to stand up and ask questions.

Cal started to turn around and explain when a metallic tap at his window caused him to freeze.

Slowly looking around he could see the bus was surrounded by men pointing automatic weapons in their direction. More could be seen in the trees that lined the road. Keeping his hands in the open he slowly reached to the window and slid it open.

"Hello," he said cautiously.

A man stepped forward. He was wearing uniform, but Cal knew he was not regular army. He let his rifle fall against the sling that held it to his body and with his hand resting on his holster walked up to the window. He spoke softly, but his voice had a deep power that could fill his church with threats of fire and brimstone if he needed it to.

"Well hello to you, young man. I can tell from your accent you aren't from around these parts." He smiled to soften the tone. "I wonder if you could help satiate my curiosity. Just before I was about to order my men to open fire as you are in a bus with a goddam Chinese flag stuck to it, you stop and the next thing we see, you two are saluting each other and shaking hands like long-lost cousins."

He paused and peered at the rest of the passengers whose frightened faces were staring at him through the windows. "The one thing I can now tell is that you ain't from China. Which is a good thing as if you were I would be saying a brief prayer over your ungodly Communist corpses by now. Let me introduce myself first. I'm the Reverend Jackson Charles Harris."

He waved his arm around as if to indicate the others still pointing their weapons at the bus. "And I have the honor to lead the Appalachian Militia."

Relief flooded through Cal's body. The rest of the bus heard what he had said and instantly started cheering and clapping.

Cal smiled. "I'm Cal and this is my friend Gordon. We have recently been released from the camps and were on our way home until the sight of the cruise missiles flying overhead caused our guards to run away. I convinced them the best idea was to turn the bus around and head to West Virginia."

The reverend raised his voice slightly to be heard over the noise still coming from the bus. "Why West Virginia, son?"

"I'm trying to find Captain Troy Gardner."

At the mention of Troy's name the reverend's eyes went wide with shock. "Now just how in the hell do you know him?"

"I was the one he sent into the camps to send back the information needed to help liberate them, sir."

CHAPTER EIGHT

COBRA, DOWNING STREET, LONDON

Adriene Winslet sat back and absorbed what the general had just said. Like a walker, high on the mountains when the clouds lift, she could see clearly now.

Her previous decisions had been based on fear and trying to do what she thought was the best for the country that was reeling and falling into anarchy, its citizens fearful about running out of food and World War Three starting. She had been blinded to the true picture and her other cabinet members and aides in the majority had been suffering from the same blinkeredness.

The general had tried to put his proposals forward before, but she had dismissed him as a warmonger, interested in securing a greater cut of the budget for the military.

She now understood that no matter what the Chinese said, food would not be arriving from the United States for a long time to come.

The minister for agriculture had confirmed what the general was saying. The reality of the situation was that even though the United Kingdom imported fifty percent of its foodstuffs, only a mere four percent of it came from the United States. The biggest portion of what the country needed came from Europe. She now understood what the phone call she received from the Chinese Premier truly meant when he said if they stayed out of the conflict then food would start flowing into the country again.

The Chinese knew the rest of Europe had no stomach for a conflict with them and would be exerting as much diplomatic and economic pressure as they could to make sure it stayed that way. And if that meant other countries using excuses about their own domestic problems as to why the exports the United Kingdom relied on had stopped, then so be it. The Chinese had most likely used those tactics to show what a formidable and ruthless enemy they were.

She looked at the cabinet ministers around the table.

"Gentlemen and ladies, we will prepare for war. I must go and see Her Majesty. After that I will address the nation and appraise them of the true situation. Their anger should not be aimed at us, but at China who is trying to redraw the world map using nuclear weapons and deceit. Hopefully that will pull everyone into line and put an end to the chaos and destruction they are causing. Ministers, go back to your offices and start to draw up plans and proposals as to how we can get this country working and feeding itself again. There must be dozens of plans drawn up by the Mandarins over the years and gathering dust."

As they began to file out, she called the general back, waiting for the room to empty until she spoke. "General, you have my apologies. Thank you for your bravery in speaking up, I know you only have the country's best interests at heart. If you could remain here I am going to call the Russian president and I will need your council."

Six Hours Later

"Prime Minister, it's remarkable, your speech has worked!" one of her ministers exclaimed. "Most of the rioting has stopped. Police forces are reporting that they fizzled out not long after your speech. But here is the incredible thing. Some got stopped not by the police, but ordinary members of the public who put themselves between the police and the rioters and basically talked them out of it."

The last hours had seemingly not only galvanized her and her ministers into action, but the whole country. The Queen had approved her plan to commit her armed forces to the fray.

After talking to the Russian president, a four-way communication between the United Kingdom, the Russians, the remnants of the United States' leadership, and Canada immediately started as to how the British could belatedly offer what resources they could bring to aid the fight.

Petrov was keeping them fully informed on the status of the US president. She had been found some hours ago and was being protected by a combination of Russian troops and local resistance fighters who were trying to get her to a safe location. Reports were sketchy as it was an ongoing situation.

General Sir Anthony Lloyd walked into the room. "Ma'am, I have just had a call from General Welch at Cheyenne Mountain. He is asking for our help on a matter," he announced jauntily.

"Of course, what is it?"

"They are currently working on how to get all the troops they have overseas back home. Apart from Japan and Korea, the biggest concentrations of their forces are here in the UK and Germany. The UK is not a problem as most of the forces are USAF and they can fly themselves out of here should they wish to. In Germany, though, they have a large contingent of ground troops and if they are going to take back their country, it's ground forces they need, not a bunch of fly boys." He paused, reaching up to rub away the threatening onset of a headache before resuming his report.

"The Germans are kicking up a right stink about allowing them to leave. Personally, I think they do not want to be seen picking sides in a war they have decided to sit out of. There is not a lot they can do about it, but the general thinks it could get ugly and he wants to, if at all possible, keep as much of what they are planning to do away from Chinese eyes and influence. He is asking to bump up the pressure to the highest level and as the president is currently indisposed, you are, so to speak, the next in line, ma'am."

She turned to an aide. "Get me the German Chancellor on the phone, please."

Ten minutes later she smiled as she put the phone down. It was not often you could disregard the niceties of official diplomatic talk and tell a fellow leader of another country what you thought of them and the consequences of standing in the way of an attempt to stop China.

She called the general back into her office. "Please call General Welch and tell him the troops will be flying to wherever he needs them, just as soon as I tell British Airways to put all their available planes at the government's disposal for the foreseeable future." As he left the room he smiled when he overheard the conversation between a few aides comparing her to Margaret Thatcher. He saw that as a good thing.

CHAPTER
NINE

BEIJING, CHINA

The generals and ministers filed into the president's office and sat down at their allocated seats around the table.

He sat at the head of table silently. None dared to look in his direction. The reports coming in from the United States over the past few hours had alarmed them all.

With the vagaries of the international clock most had gone to bed with the news that the American surrender was a formality. They were only waiting for the press and dignitaries to gather at a location being prepared so they could record their victory to be broadcast around the world.

Most were woken up by nervous aides during the night to hear the news that unknown paratroopers were landing, and missiles were bombarding various locations across a country they had been told was pacified and in their control.

The president shouted angrily and beat his fist on the table. "You told me we had won the victory of all victories."

He let that statement hang in the air. "Which one of you is going to tell me that the Russians have landed on American soil? That cruise missiles were launched from both Russian and American ships that I was informed our glorious navy would be able to keep out of range of interfering with our efforts?"

The head of the navy looked sharply up. "Sir, I informed the committee that the navy would be able to protect the fleet that is currently heading toward America. We have contained the American Pacific fleet which is leaderless anyway—our strategic strikes on Hawaii destroyed their command structure.

"The Russian fleet is another matter. We are not at war with them. My ships are keeping the ones that approach away but I must remind you that the bulk of our ships are concentrated around the invasion fleet. It is impossible to track all of the ships that could pose a threat."

The president sat, his eyes looking around everyone in the room. "Yet still they fight back. Someone is leading them. They may be contained but don't any of you think that their naval inactivity is due to the fact they are biding their time, rebuilding their strength, waiting for most opportune moment to fight back?" He paused, waiting to see if anyone was following his logic. "Are you so simple, you think that because we have crippled their command structure they will sit there and do nothing? The snake will grow a new head soon. You have failed to take their command center buried under the mountain. I was assured we would be able to. We need that facility if we are to control the country and its nuclear weapons. Then the rest of the world will quake in the shadow we will cast over them. From all your initial success, all I am getting now is failure."

Eyes were averted as no one wanted to take responsibility for that failure. "This victory needs to be quick and absolute, the whole plan relies on it."

Leaning forwards, he asked the room, "I do not want to hear your excuses about these setbacks. They are just bee stings that hurt us briefly but will not stop us. When will the surrender be signed?"

No one could look him in the eye. "What are you not telling me?" he snapped when he saw the sudden uncomfortable movements of shame and knowledge around some at the table. He pointed at the general in overall command of the ground forces. "You. Tell me now!"

"Sir," the general quailed slightly but tried to maintain his composure. "The President of the United States is currently unaccounted for. In the chaos of the Russian invasion contact has been lost with Agent Fen Shu who was escorting her to the surrender ceremony. Our soldiers are scouring the city and we are pouring more in. The Russians are too few in number to hold out for long. Soon we will have wiped them all out and we will find where they sought shelter. I assure you she has a strong protection force chosen from the very best. They are safe somewhere that unfortunately they cannot communicate from."

"My niece is missing?"

The room looked up in shock. They all knew that Fen Shu was his niece, but it had never been officially acknowledged before.

The president flew into a rage. "You lose the president, you lose my niece, what else are you going to lose next? The United States of America? That cannot be allowed to happen." He seethed in silence as he fought to control his anger and deliver his orders.

"Advance the invasion plans. Send more soldiers. The enemy is fighting back, and they are getting help. We must end this before more decide to turn against us and join in. If any areas become too troublesome target them with another nuclear launch. They must learn the consequences of daring to defy us. Now get out and deliver to me the victory you promised."

The generals and ministers raced to the door to be first out of the room, lest they fall under the scrutiny of their president again. The plan they had all thought foolproof was falling apart. Their careers, their country, and their own lives depended on it succeeding. No cost was too great to make it happen. Orders were immediately sent out mobilizing more divisions. Any ships that were still available were ordered to the nearest ports to enable embarkation.

The North Korean divisions, ready and waiting for orders from their Chinese masters, were commanded to set sail immediately from the ports where they had been quietly massing right under the continual scrutiny of the South Koreans and the Americans. The navy pleaded with them that it would be unwise to undertake such a task without a surface and underwater fleet for protection. The vessels would be as good as defenseless as they crossed the vast Pacific Ocean.

Those pleas fell on deaf ears. They had been given orders and they were to be followed.

The admiral in charge of the navy, still smarting from the dressing down from the president, began to understand that the fingers of blame would immediately point to him if the next wave of the invasion stalled. As the president had pointed out, they had crippled the navy's command structure, but not the navy itself. The vastly powerful American Pacific fleet was still out there, licking their wounds. He knew they were there somewhere, but they had disappeared; steaming south into the vastness of the still, in places, uncharted Southern Pacific Ocean.

The American submarines were also still out there somewhere. The Los Angeles-class, Sea Wolf, and Virginia-class fast attack submarines, that the Chinese had spent billions of dollars on developing measures to find and track after they had goaded the Chinese many times by appearing when least expected, had not been detected since this began. They were out there somewhere and no matter how many times the admiral explained it to his leaders, if they did not want to be found, they wouldn't be. The Ohio-class ballistic missile submarines, each capable individually of bringing complete nuclear devastation to his country, were doing what they were designed to do: waiting silently, lurking undetected in the dark depths below the surface for the order to launch a counterattack.

They were called a deterrent for good reason. The fact that they might or might not be just over the horizon, fully capable to reign death down from the skies at a single verified command was enough to strike fear into the bravest man. It was why the Chinese had invested hundreds of billions of dollars to increase their own detection and deterrent capabilities. Building more vessels and submarines. Stealing or at times developing their own technology to catch up with their great enemies' capabilities. But no matter how impressive it all looked, all they were doing was playing catch up. The Americans and the Russians were continually developing weapons to keep themselves ahead in the game.

The cost of the failure they would accuse him of would be quick. A brief trial and then a bullet to the brain, with his family given the final insult of being charged for the bullet.

He secretly began making plans to ensure his own survival. Being head of the navy gave him control over all the industries that built, fed, equipped, and clothed it. The tribute he naturally and was expected to skim off the top, had made him a wealthy man. Not that he needed the money whilst he held the position. His position provided him with houses, servants, and his own personal jet and ship so he could tour his command at ease and in comfort.

If he lost his position though, the wealth he had created would enable him and his family to live in opulent comfort for the rest of their days in some safe country, far from the reach of Chinese influence. Living long enough to enjoy it was his only concern.

He'd gathered a few trusted aids, members of his own family he had given important roles to through nothing but self-serving nepotism. They all relied on him for their positions and future well-being, so their loyalty was unquestionable. Plans were made so he and his family could escape from the country at a moment's notice. Access to his wealth was no problem. All he would need was a trip to his private bank in Switzerland.

The general in overall charge of the ground forces, as soon as he left the meeting, issued orders to be sent to his regional commanders in the United States.

The commanders of five of the six regions that the Chinese had divided America into received those orders. They were to advance their plans for controlling the local population. Though these hastily drafted orders were confusing to those who received them; they had been following the plan. The camps were quietly ridding the invaders of the excess population that were deemed unnecessary for their victory. The old and the infirmed were succumbing in great numbers to the virus. Their control was increasing geographically as an ever-growing number of cities, towns, and villages were garrisoned by their troops, spreading the supposed humanitarian aid they brought secured by soldiers, who immediately began the real mission of subjugation.

Some did nothing, unable to see how they could do more than they were already doing at the current time. More soldiers were needed, and they would arrive soon, so they waited.

Others more eager to please divided their forces more to advance the program. They reasoned that if one hundred soldiers could take a town then fifty would just have to work harder to achieve the same goal. The Chinese net of control did accelerate in places, but it left them dangerously weakened and exposed.

One commander, with a more brutal streak, accelerated his extermination program. He had interpreted his orders that way. He needed to control the population, take away their strength, make them unable to revolt. Tens of thousands of captured military personnel, law enforcement officers, and anyone deemed to potentially be more of a threat than a help were in camps or former prisons emptied of their inmates, who lay in shallow mass graves close by.

They were fed a carefully controlled, barely edible diet to further weaken and control them.

The sick lying in hospitals or temporary aid stations set up in school gymnasiums or other large halls, had already started to be dealt with. They were going to die anyway so wasting manpower and resources on them was not efficient. The buildings were sealed up and once the last soldier had left, canisters containing poison gas were thrown in and the doors barred. He ordered the extermination of other camps. Not all of them, though, as they did provide the forced labor needed to clear up the damage caused by the aerial bombardment. The inmates of these camps were continually fed the lie that the work was necessary to help the humanitarian effort that the gracious Chinese government was providing.

Whole camps, under the command of this one brutal commander went to sleep in their squalid quarters never to see another dawn.

The sixth region did nothing. Its commander had been sentenced to die by firing squad and the agent who had yet to appoint his replacement was currently bound hand and foot with the president of the United States pointing a gun at her head.

CHAPTER
TEN

KENTUCKY

Leland, sat in a cabin deep in the Kentucky wilderness in the foot-hills of Black Mountain, felt secure for the first time since his escape from New York and his long and perilous journey to get to the place he knew well.

Secure but angry.

He had tried to reach Pittsburgh. There were Movement soldiers there who could help them. Having barely escaped New York before the bombs fell, he and the two former marines that had stuck with him, had nothing more than the weapons they carried and the magazines to feed them on their persons. They needed supplies and equipment and Pittsburgh was the nearest place he knew he could get them.

After stealing a truck at gunpoint, they had headed west. The sight of three heavily armed and dangerously mean-looking bat-tle-scarred men helped their journey. Stealing fuel and food from citizens who, if they tried to resist, were shot out of hand, they headed towards Pittsburgh. After approaching a roadblock out-side the city, he realized they could go no further. Expecting it to be manned by a US military or even better a local militia, they approached slowly but confidently. After all, what did they have to fear?

Too late he saw that the soldiers approaching were wearing uniforms he never expected to see even on American soil.

Not waiting to find out why soldiers from the People's Re-public of China were walking toward him, he slammed the truck into reverse and ordered his travelling companions to open fire. Incoming fire began to strike the truck as soon as the soldiers re-alized he was moving away from them. A line of bullets stitched the windscreen, the pain of a bullet creasing his skull making him scream in pain and anger as he ploughed the truck at full speed in reverse through the cars and debris that were littering the road. Fighting to keep the semi from jack-knifing, he kept trying to put as much distance as he could between them and their assailants.

Bullets sparked and ricocheted as they struck the cab. Cobb, one of his travelling companions, was leaning from the passenger window firing magazine after magazine toward the enemy. Not in any real expectation of hitting any of them, but in the hope that the volume of lead he was putting down range would disturb their aim. As the distance increased the number of bullets hitting their receding target diminished proportionately. Concentrating fully on driving, he heard a scream of pain from beside him, but could not give it a moment's thought. If he took his eye off the mirrors, he knew within seconds he would lose control and it would all be over.

Rounding a bend, he knew they were out of the line of sight as the incoming fire dropped to zero. He slowed the truck and risked a glance at the others. Cobb was still leaning out of the window, his rifle held ready, but his other companion was slumped in his seat, both hands held to his throat trying to stem the flow of blood that pumped from a wound in his neck. He slammed the brakes on the truck, skidding it to a stop in a cloud of burning rubber. Reaching over and pulling his hands away from his throat, he examined the wound. Arterial blood spurted out, spraying the shattered windscreen. He knew straight away the wound, without immediate medical attention, was a killer. The man was drowning in his own blood as it filled his lungs, whilst the rest pumped out through his fingers as his hands desperately tried to stop it from leaving his body.

He looked forwards, steam and smoke from burning oil rose from under the hood. The engine block sticking out in front of them had absorbed most of the incoming fire, but it had paid the price. The truck was terminally damaged. Ignoring his dying companion by his side he wiped his own blood that was pouring down his face and engaged reverse again. The truck moved, but the smoke and steam billowing from under the hood increased and it began screeching and grinding as the engine started to tear itself apart.

Keeping his foot to the floor Leland coaxed every yard he could out of the dying truck. Distance was their only safety margin and the more of it the better. Within minutes flames began licking out from under the hood and he knew it was time to abandon it. Before it had stopped and not even checking or caring if his wounded companion was alive, he ordered Cobb to gather the unfortunate man's weapons and magazines and prepare to abandon the truck.

The pursuit would be coming and there was no time to waste.

Before leaping from the cab, he glanced at the man beside him. The last of his lifeblood had left him and his unseeing eyes stared ahead, the panic and pain still showing on his slack features. Showing a rare moment of compassion, Leland closed his eyes and said a silent prayer for his soul, thanking him for the service he had given to his country before pulling a missed pistol magazine from his vest, and joining Cobb who was kneeling at the front of the now burning vehicle, his rifle pointing toward where they expected any moment for the pursuit to arrive from.

"Come on, Cobb, lets hightail it out of here."

By the time they reached the tree line, racing engines could be heard approaching. Half a punishing hour later, Leland held up his hand to indicate to the man who had kept on his heels,

73

following him through the dense woods, that he was stopping. They had come far enough and fast enough to be way ahead of any pursuing force.

Unable to speak, both men slumped to the floor, chests pumping as they tried to get as much oxygen as they could into their lungs. Leland, fitter than men half his age, waited for Cobb to stop retching before handing him a water bottle.

"What now, Gunny?" Cobb eventually managed to gasp.

"Son, I hate to fucking say it, but I think we've been had. Whatever Butler and the Movement planned it certainly didn't include aerial bombing New York and having Commu-fucking Chinese bastards on United States soil. This puts us in a tricky situation. We started this with our few pissant bombs and taking down the stock exchange. *But* the next thing we know, nukes and other ordnance are reigning down on the States and now we are being shot at by Commies."

He paused as he remembered a sight he thought he would never see. A mushroom cloud rising on the distant horizon in the direction of D.C.

"The enemy we were fighting was the government, but now it looks like they are going to need every patriot left to fight an invasion. Whatever we think about them, I think our reenlistment papers have just landed, delivered by an AK-powered Chinese bullet, and I for one am going to sign them. We were the American resistance and now it looks like we are the United States resistance.

"Semper Fi, Gunny. I'm with you all the way."

Leland nodded at Cobb. "I still want to get back to my Kentucky boys. There is no way they are going down without a fight, and as I have said before, if they are snug in their hollers I'd put a hundred of them up against a whole division of Chinese bastards. But firstly, I want to see who we are up against. If it is an invasion, then they will be going for the big cities first."

He checked his compass and pointed west. "Pittsburgh is the nearest and the only big city anywhere near our route south." He stood and checked his weapon. "Are you up for a little recon mission, Cobb?"

In response the old marine stood up, checked, and with a pull, charged his weapon and said, "Lead on, Gunny. You just tell me when I can start killing those Communist fuckers."

"Don't worry, son, I have a feeling there will be plenty to go around soon enough."

Twelve hours later the two men had slipped past the roadblocks and checkpoints that circled the city and, using their years of training, worked their way into a position on Mount Washington—the hill-cum-suburb that afforded an elevated view over downtown Pittsburgh. They found a concealed spot to observe from and whilst Cobb kept guard, Leland kept up a quiet commentary as he watched through his binoculars. What was left of the city was clearly under Chinese control. The city itself beyond the river had been destroyed by the nuclear blast. The skeletons and remains of the high-rise city center buildings were a stark reminder of the power humankind had harnessed when creating such a devastating weapon. The damage, though, did not extend to a wide radius.

The large parking lot below them on the banks of the river had been turned into a containment center. The buildings around it were scorched and flattened but beyond it, and on the hills leading up to where they observed from, the damage reduced greatly the further out the distance. Thousands of citizens were held behind rows of razor wire coils, guarded by soldiers wearing cumbersome radiation suits.

"They must have dialed back the yield on whatever bomb they aimed here," Leland mused out loud. "But it looks to me as if the bastards are deliberately poisoning the people they are rounding up. Why else would they be holding them there? The radiation levels must be high enough to warrant the guards to wear protective gear but not citizens."

Leland was almost right. The yield of the weapon had not been reduced deliberately; the device had failed to explode correctly and instead had fizzled out. The Chinese had sent a team of observers to investigate the success of the blast and had discovered not a complete city lying in ruins with millions of dead, but only a small area of destruction around ground zero. Extra troops had urgently been diverted from other areas to contain and process the hundreds of thousands of civilians they did not expect to have to deal with. Callously they decided to let the bomb that should have killed them do the job for them, albeit more slowly and painfully. They left the people exposed to the still-lethally high levels of radiation in the area. The citizens of Pittsburgh were not part of the plan, so needed to be disposed of.

Leland snorted in disgust. "The roadblocks we have seen are not to stop anyone getting in, they are stopping anyone escaping. Then they round them up, get them as close to the blast as they can and let the radiation do the rest."

He observed trucks continually drive up and disgorge more citizens who were herded into the camp. What shocked him were the armored and other vehicles the Chinese were using. They were US military.

"Goddamn bastards are using our own stuff against us. They must have hit the National Guard barracks."

A few hours of observation were all that was needed. The Chinese had complete control over the remains of city and were rounding up all its occupants. The fact that they were using US vehicles meant any force capable of resisting had been wiped out in the first phases of the attack, leaving the citizens defenseless. The captors were not benevolent either. Knowingly letting them absorb what would most likely be a lethal dose of radiation was not enough. A disturbance attracted his attention. Three men wearing military uniform fought back when the guards tried to separate them from women and children, presumably their families.

They were pulled to the floor by an overpowering number of guards and subjected to a vicious beating. Once order was restored, an officer walked up to the three men who now had their hands bound and were kneeling in a row. Without hesitation he drew his sidearm and shot all three in the head. The guards then ordered other civilians to pick their bodies up and throw them unceremoniously into the river.

Having seen enough and concerned about exposing themselves to the radiation, the two men began to make their escape from the city. Using a different route out and near to the edge of its limits they came across an entrance to a neighborhood that was barricaded with cars and heavy furniture. Entering the rear of a house that was a few hundred yards away over an open area of grass, they observed what was going on.

The neighborhood had, by the looks of it, decided to band together to defend themselves. Men and women with a variety of weapons were standing guard. Both could see the defenses were not built by anyone with military experience. Though they did not have a lot to work with, what they had constructed was better than nothing if you were trying to defend yourself.

"Shall we go see if they can give us any intelligence? We should warn them about the radiation as well," said Cobb.

"I don't see why not. They may even have a car they can loan us," Leland said with a wry chuckle. The last vehicle Leland had 'borrowed' was the truck and that had taken a bullet through the window to seal the deal.

Leland stood up, but Cobb grabbed his arm and pulled him down.

"Listen!" was all he said.

Leland strained his ears. A distant rumble of heavy engines could faintly be heard. Cobb pointed up to the sky, a small object was hovering high overhead.

"Gunny, look up. I think they are using drones."

Even though he followed Cobbs' finger upwards his eyesight was not good enough to spot the distant hovering object.

"I'll have to take your word for it," he grumbled. "The issue for us now is most likely those engines are heading this way. The defenses won't hold up to a peashooter let alone anything heavier. Let's go warn them, they may have chance to disperse and escape."

Again, they stood up, but Cobb pulled Leland down again. They were too late, a hummer with an armored cupola mounting a fifty-caliber machine gun drove rapidly down the street. It was still bearing National Guard markings and flying the Stars and Stripes from its aerial.

Both immediately saw that the uniforms on the soldiers inside the vehicle were not American. They also were not wearing radiation suits and the men took some comfort from that. If the

Chinese were not making their soldiers wear them then the levels must be low enough. The civilians in the barricade could not tell the difference and began cheering thinking help had arrived at last.

More lined the barricade as the cheering attracted others from the community. Both men watched from the darkened interior of the room. When the cupola started to rotate and point toward the barricade they knew with dreaded certainty what was going to happen next.

Cobb raised his weapon, but Leland slapped it down. "There ain't nothing we can do, Cobb. Sorry to say but this isn't our fight. And anyway, what the hell can we do against an armored Hummer?"

The cheering of the crowd subsided when more vehicles drove up to join the first. No one had emerged from the vehicles to acknowledge the welcome the community was giving them. As the latest arrival's turrets rotated toward the puny barricade, the community realized all may not be as expected.

Panicked shouting now replaced the elation they had all felt moments before. Some fled from the barricade whilst others bravely raised their weapons.

The raising of weapons against them was the trigger the Chinese may have been waiting for. The community before them changed from non-threatening to threatening with that action. The three Hummers opened fire. The bullets, with the power to penetrate light armor and capable of reducing buildings to rubble, threw a devastating hail of heavy lead at the makeshift barricade. The brave but unfortunate defenders stood no chance.

Leland and Cobb watched with morbid fascination as some of the defenders futilely fired their weapons at their attackers. The human body is a fragile thing and when hit at close range with such a powerful and heavy object as a fifty-caliber bullet, the kinetic energy displaced produces devastating results. Bodies disintegrated, the fine red mist that sprayed from them staying in the air longer than the unrecognizable lumps of raw flesh and bone that were thrown back from the wall of cars and furniture.

The barricade, unable to stand against such power for more than a few seconds was reduced to lumps of metal and splinters. A heavier armored vehicle arrived and drove straight through the remains, followed by the Hummers.

They watched as the convoy drove on into the neighborhood. People tried to surrender, holding their hands up in the universal sign of submission but that did not stop them from continuing to spread death. Not satisfied, squads of soldiers dismounted from more vehicles that arrived and, covered by the smoking barrels of the machine guns, went house to house, dragging those who had tried to hide outside.

The message was clear. If you defy them, then your life is forfeit. The cowering, terrified families were executed as soon as they were discovered. Man, woman, or child; it did not matter to the soldiers. Darkness was falling when the Chinese left, content that no one was left alive.

Leland and Cobb had not spoken for hours. Their anger and rage at what they had witnesses too powerful to put into words. Silently they waited for the last engine noise to fade into silence before exiting the house and continuing their journey on foot.

Immediately after this, Leland experienced a paradigm shift in his attitude to his fellow Americans. Before this, they were part of the problem. In his opinion, they blindly followed the false government, giving it validity by accepting everything it did, and paying the taxes (without thought) that gave the powerful the resources to further control them.

Before this shift, he would have (and had without any guilt ever), robbed, killing if necessary, anyone who stood in the way of what he wanted. Now, every American was on the same side as him. His role as a fighter meant he was their protector too.

Using back roads, they found abandoned vehicles at houses or along the roadside. They drove until they ran out of fuel. The route they picked took them away from all population centers, but at times it was unavoidable. To their surprise the two mean-looking, heavily armed veterans were welcomed at small towns and villages. These remote places had yet to see any of the invaders, but they knew they may be coming. The television stations, under Chinese control, were broadcasting propaganda they just didn't believe. One minute bombs were falling, and the next all was okay, and the benevolent Chinese had arrived to offer humanitarian aid.

These Americans offered them food and shelter, desperate to hear their news. Leland realized these communities could form the backbone of the Movement. The militias were well armed and capable, but numbers would be their biggest issue. There were not enough of them to take on the Chinese. These communities would provide the numbers to turn the militias into an army.

Leland told them everything he knew and had since discovered, though deliberately missing out his part in the beginning. Playing heavily on the inhuman nature of what they were facing, he left them with no uncertain knowledge of what would happen if they bowed to the will of the invaders.

The further south they journeyed the more communities they sought out to spread the seeds of rebellion. It was as General Liu had predicted: the Chinese tactics of oppression were feeding the sparks of rebellion and the flame was growing brighter.

Walking up a track in the foothills of Black Mountain, Cobb and Leland were alert and aware of their surroundings. A voice hidden in the deep bush ahead made them crouch instantly. They did not raise their weapons, however, as they knew to do so would signal instant lead-filled death.

"Well hi there, stranger. You sure are a mighty long ways from anywhere. Are ya'll lost?"

Leland called back, "I ain't lost at all. I'm Gunnery Sergeant Leland Pullen with Corporal Cobb here by my side, reckon you need some help in fighting some Chinese ticks that are latching on and sucking the blood from some fine American beef."

The bush parted and a man stepped out wearing camouflage and a tactical vest adorned with magazines for the AR-15 he carried. "Gunny! That you?"

He squinted at Leland who was still crouching, holding his hands away from his weapons. He laughed and raised his voice. "Lower your weapons boys, we have the legend that is Gunny Pullen in our midst."

He waved for them to stand.

"Let's get you back to the command cabin. I'm sure they are going to be mighty glad to see you."

CHAPTER ELEVEN

TEXAS

Driving fast and with purpose, the ruse worked and General Liu left the suburbs of San Antonio. No checkpoint stopped them. The guards reasoned it was natural for a staff car containing a high-ranking official to be fleeing the noises of battle emanating from the city.

Turning off a main road they sped along a few miles of rural roads that eventually changed from tarmac to dirt. At the next checkpoint his car slowed to a stop, surprising him. The checkpoint was manned by Americans, some in uniform, most not, but all carrying weapons.

From the lack of surprise at seeing a car bearing Chinese flags, it was clear they were expected. Tommy Cho, now adjusted to his real name, had told Liu little on the journey apart from that he was a sergeant in the United States Army who had infiltrated the Chinese invaders when they first arrived. His luck held, and he had found himself attached to the headquarters group where his English skills had led to him being assigned as Liu's aid.

Sergeant Cho spoke briefly to the guard at the checkpoint before being waved through. He followed the road which ended outside a large house. More guards were visible on the wide veranda that ran along the front of the property as he opened the general's car door and led him inside. It was a hive of activity which stopped when the general, wearing his uniform, entered.

A man walked toward him and held out his hand which the general automatically took and shook. The man spoke to him in perfect Mandarin. "General, welcome. Thankfully we got you out of there just in time. When we got the report yesterday of what had happened to you, we knew we had to act."

Taken aback at being addressed in his native language, he covered his shock and to counter, replied in English. Not as perfect, but understandable. "Is it you I must thank for saving my life?"

The man shook his head and chuckled. "I think the main thanks should go to Sergeant Cho, but yes, I played a part in organizing it."

General Liu snapped to attention and saluted. He pulled his gun from its holster and reversed it before handing it grip first to the man. "Please accept my surrender."

In reply the man saluted smartly. "Sebastian Walker at your

service, sir. I think you misunderstand; we do not want your surrender. We need your help to end this war."

The general bristled indignantly. "I will never betray my country. I have offered my surrender and expect to be treated as your military code sets out."

Sebastian held his arms up in a calming gesture. "Please, General, let me explain. Cho has reported that you are an honorable soldier who tried to help American citizens when you discovered what certain branches of your government had done. It was as abhorrent to you as it is to us.

"I suspect, General, that if you were in complete control then the job to free our country would be a whole lot more difficult. You would have been a worthy adversary, but now we want to make you an honorable friend. You are shrewd enough to realize that you will ultimately lose this war. If it was waged differently as you well know you probably would be close to winning total victory by now.

"You have not secured our nuclear arsenal, nor ever will. Our allies are preparing and when the time is right we will strike. The American nation is hurt but not beaten. You miscalculated who you were dealing with—"

General Liu interrupted him, "Mister Sebastian Walker you are right. Many times I tried to make my superiors listen to sense, but more powerful voices than mine prevailed. But I repeat, I have surrendered and will never betray my country."

Sebastian handed his pistol back. "I do not wish to accept your surrender, sir. I want your help to save your country from total annihilation, because if your country continues on the path it has chosen then that will happen. I am sure you want that to happen far less than most." Sebastian turned as someone called out to him.

Turning back, he continued. "If you would excuse me, sir. I have an urgent matter I must attend to. If you could remain under the care of Sergeant Cho until I return, we can continue our conversation. And I believe others far above my paygrade will want to talk to you too."

"Of course, Mister Walker, I understand. But before you go could you tell me what branch of your government you work for?"

Sebastian replied in perfect Mandarin, "Please, call me Sebastian. And I no longer work for the government, sir. I am the concierge at the Waldorf Astoria hotel in New York."

Stunned into silence Liu watched Sebastian don body armor that someone brought to him and run out the door to join a convoy of cars and pickup trucks that sped off down the dirt track.

Liu accepted a coffee and a chair from his former aide. Sipping it, he looked at Cho. "A Concierge! I now fully understand why we will never win."

CHAPTER TWELVE

SAN ANTONIO

The Russian troops had moved Madeline and the bound Fen Shu into the kitchen area of the café and were hard at work fortifying their position.

A captain, who spoke excellent English, was assigned to protect her along with his platoon of battle-hardened elite troops. Stripping a bulletproof vest and ballistic helmet from one of the dead Chinese soldiers outside, he washed the blood from them and requested politely that Madeline put them on. Once she had, she slung one of the bodyguard's compact sub machine guns over her shoulder and picked up the handgun, holding it firmly.

The captain nodded at her in respect. Fully aware of who he was assigned to protect he kept her up to date with the situation. The plan was simple: once she had been located, the troops rushed to her position and created a secure cordon to await transport out of the city.

As the Russians disengaged from fighting the Chinese troops and pulled back to her location, a silence descended over the city that had previously echoed with the sound of automatic rifle fire and explosions.

"Captain, how are we getting out of here?" Tanner asked in a strong voice designed to show everyone listening that she was in charge.

"Madam President, the American resistance will provide us with transport. They know we have located you and they are on their way."

"What about the Chinese, won't they have something to say about that?"

"Yes, they will," the Russian officer replied equably, "and I do not suggest that this will be an easy thing we do. There are few of us and many of them. We hit as much of their command network and troop concentrations as we could identify as we were jumping in. The units we initially engaged were already caught unawares and were overcome with relative ease. I imagine currently they are pouring more troops into the area to try to wipe us out. They are not an army of conscription and the soldiers we will be against will be their very best. So no, Madam President, we are, as the saying goes, 'not out of the wood yet.'"

She glanced down at the pistol in her hand with evident meaning. "Well, I won't let go of this then."

Fen Shu had overheard this and began shouting obscenities at them in both English and Mandarin. But she fell silent and her face showed real fear when Madeline turned to her.

"Oh sweetie, have no fear. If we are about to be overrun I will save the last bullet for you. There is no way you are escaping the justice that is coming your way. Captain? Gag her, please."

The captain smiled and ordered two of his men to hold down the wildly fighting woman, so he could stuff a rag in her mouth and hold it in place with the tape he roughly wound around her head. Her struggles immediately ceased as she fought for breath through the blood that had clotted in her recently broken nose.

The captain smiled as her face turned bright red with the effort. "Don't worry," he added with professional cruelty, "we will not let her die. Yet..."

Chapter

Thirteen

Half an hour later the captain listened to an incoming message coming through his headset and turned to Madeline.

"Madam President. The transport will soon be here. Please, we must get ready to depart the moment they arrive." Walking to the front of the shop she could see hundreds of Russian paratroopers all with weapons raised, utilizing all available cover to defend her from the enemy they expected to appear from any quadrant.

Out of sight to the left, gunshots rang out as the defenders exchanged fire with Chinese troops who were probing and trying to break through the solid ring of defense around her location.

She was surprised at the numbers and knew there were probably more in positions she could not see. "Are they sending enough transport for all of us?" Tanner asked.

"I do not know, Madam President, but we will find out when they arrive I expect," the hulking Russian replied before laughing briefly. "I am a fan of your American movies *Black Hawks Down.*

We can always run the San Antonio mile. Anything you Americans can do, us Russians can do better." He stood taller as he bragged, puffing his chest in self-belief. "But do not have the fear; we will all get out of this city one way or another."

She smiled at his humor and patted his arm. "I hope it does not come to that, Captain."

Ten minutes later more gunshots could be heard in the distance. As the minutes wore away the sounds of gunfire got closer. The distant sounds of battle began to increase in tempo until it was continuous.

The captain, now with a worried look on his face, approached Madeline. "Madam President, we have hit a problem. The transport is heavily engaged with a strong opposing force and are unable to proceed any further. It is recommended by my superiors that we proceed to their location and render assistance."

He expected her to falter after telling her they were going to confront more danger if they were to get out of the city, but again she surprised him. Tightening the strap on the helmet that was too large for her, so it did not keep falling forward covering her eyes, she pushed the handgun she was holding into a strap on her body armor and reached for the small stubby machine gun that hung from a strap around her shoulders.

Inspecting it briefly, she found and pressed the button that ejected its magazine, checked it and reinserted it into place, and pulled the charging handle. "Let's go. The longer we wait the more of those brave people who are trying to rescue us will die."

A senior officer approached and spoke rapidly in Russian to the captain.

"This is Major Egorov, he is asking for me to make translate of instructions to you."

Madeline shook the major's hand with a nod of greeting and listened as the captain translated.

The captain would escort her in the center of a tight knot of his men. The rest of his force would form more circles of protection radiating out from her position. If they engaged in a firefight, which they fully expected, she would lie on the ground and the captain and his men's sole job would be to put their bodies in the way of her and the danger.

He apologized in advance if she might be manhandled roughly but emphasized that her safety was his primary, secondary, and tertiary concern. She smiled at his seriousness.

Five minutes later, with every soldier fully briefed and in position, they set out toward the source of the firing that still echoed through the city streets. Fen Shu was manhandled to her feet by two soldiers. They kept her hands bound behind her back but untied her feet.

Moving at a fast walking pace Madeline could see little through the phalanx of soldiers that surrounded her. The two flanking her both kept a hand on the drag handle on the back of her body armor, to both stop her stumbling and to help her keep up the pace. Her inability to speak Russian did not stop her understanding the meanings of the short conversations and short one-word sentences shouted between the group surrounding her, as orders were given, or as a soldier tripped or stumbled.

Gunfire close by made the soldiers surrounding her stop. She could not tell if it came from the Chinese or Russians, but as the volume increased, she knew it was coming from both sides. With no warning the two holding her drag handle pushed her roughly to the floor. A weight pressing on her back made her realize one was using his knee to hold her down. She lay on the floor holding her gun in her hands, listening to the sounds of battle raging around her.

In her political career she had attended countless meetings, visited numerous bases, and sat on many committees which were concerned with the armed forces. She had listened to many reports regarding skirmishes, small-scale fights and large battles, which the soldiers of the United States had been involved in over the years. As a consequence, she thought she knew what the modern soldier had to endure in battle.

She realized she had no idea what it was really like at all. The firing, shouting, screaming, and utter confusion could never be portrayed in a report read by a bored aide. The fear was also something you could not begin to imagine as you went into sensory overload, your brain trying to cope with so many things going on at once. Coupled with the fact a bullet could end your life at any second, she found it the most terrifying, but at the same time the most exhilarating experience of her entire life.

She had listened to soldiers when they explained that when the bullets start flying, you are no longer fighting for your country, but for your brothers in arms who are beside you, fighting just as hard as you to stay alive, to get back to family and loved ones. She had nodded her politically trained head and put a compassionate look on her face to show she understood.

Now she actually understood what they meant. She was surrounded by soldiers from another country who had parachuted into a nation they had trained to fight. Not as conquerors, but liberators, all fighting as hard as each other just to stay alive. These soldiers, ordered by their government to parachute into a city most had never heard of before they looked at a map, to attempt to rescue her, were just fighting to stay alive.

A soldier kneeling in front of her screamed in pain and fell backwards holding his hands to his leg. Blood began pouring from between his fingers as he tried to stem the flow from the wound. She did not need to understand the one-word sentence his comrades kept repeating at the tops of their voices: they were calling for a medic.

Unable to move with the soldier still kneeling on her back Madeline reached out with her arm to attempt to offer the soldier help. Frustrated at the helplessness she felt at only being able to pat his leg to offer him comfort, she decided she needed to do more.

She pushed upwards and with a shout of annoyance, the soldier kneeling on her back was unbalanced. She turned and stopped him pushing her back down by holding her hand up and then pointing toward the injured man. He immediately understood that she wanted to help.

He nodded in agreement and as she crawled toward the stricken man, he crouched next to her covering as much of her as he could with his own body. Her mind dragged up memories of a first aid course she had attended long ago but as she looked at the blood-soaked trousers covering the soldier's leg, she knew his injury went far beyond the simple bandaging and wound dressing she had been taught.

A soldier next to her shoved an aid kit he'd pulled from one of his pouches into her hands. Ripping it open she pulled the soldier's hands away from his wound and, using scissors from the kit, cut the trousers to inspect it.

The wound was not spurting blood which she took as a good sign. Not understanding the writing on the packages within the kit she ripped a few open until she found a large wound dressing which she pressed against the ragged hole in the man's leg and wound a bandage tightly around it.

The bandages soon changed red and blood began dripping from them indicating her efforts had not stopped the bleeding. To her relief the medic arrived, pushing through her surrounding guards. His uniform, hands, and face were stained with blood from his previous patients.

He took one look at what she had done then pulled a tourniquet from his bag and applied it above the wound. As he finished and was closing his bag he looked at Madeline and said, "Good work." Then as quick as he arrived he was gone.

Madeline had been concentrating on her task so hard, the sounds of fighting had faded into the background, but they returned to full volume when the captain shouted at her to get ready to move.

Helping the wounded soldier to his feet she put her arm around his shoulder to support him as they began moving again. The men around her continually fired their weapons as they fought their way through any opposition they encountered. Her world shrunk to the small area around her as she put all her efforts into helping the wounded man until, at a shouted command, the knot of men surrounding her stopped.

Gently helping the man to the ground, he kept repeating the only Russian word she understood, "Spasibo," meaning 'thank you.'

Her phalanx of guard parted briefly to admit the captain to its protected core. "We wait here, Madam President. The convoy is close. The major is preparing to attack. When it is successful we will proceed."

"Thank you, Captain. And dare I ask what we do if it is not successful?"

He gave Madeline a big smile. "Then we get the chance to do the San Antonio mile!"

Madeline helped the injured soldier back up and they moved against the wall of a large building and waited. Abruptly the sound of gunfire increased to a crescendo of firing and explosions as more than two hundred Russian paratroopers joined in the fray.

For over five minutes the battle raged until it finally began to peter out. After listening to his radio, the captain turned to her.

"The Chinese are defeated; the area is clear. We are finishing to make checks of the area and we will be on our way."

She breathed a sigh of relief. The men around her also relaxed slightly, still with their weapons held ready but exchanging a few smiles and back slaps with their comrades in arms. Madeline stood up to see the major approaching with a civilian by his side. They were conversing in Russian. As soon as he spotted her the civilian stopped talking, let the weapon he was carrying fall to his side, and saluted.

"Madam President, my name is Sebastian. If you are ready shall we get you to somewhere safer?"

"Thank you, Sebastian, for coming to get us. Tell me, are you the leader of the local resistance or military?"

"No, Madam, I am neither. I am the concierge at the Waldorf

Astoria hotel in New York."

For once stunned into silence she helped the injured Russian soldier to his feet and, still holding a gun in one hand, walked toward the waiting transport.

CHAPTER FOURTEEN

HOLLY RIVER BASE, WV

Bear Grayson took off his headset and turned to the men in the room. "Steve, your wife is out of San Antonio and in a safe place. Getting her to a secure location is now priority number one."

Steve slumped back in his chair, relief washing over his face. "I need to get to her."

Gus slapped him on his back. "Trust me, Steve. Whatever you think, you will be way down on the list of who wants to see her."

Captain Troy Gardner sat thinking silently. Since returning from the aborted mission to release the prisoners from the camp at Caldwell where he and his men had seen the missiles streaking overhead, he had sat brooding as all the coordinated attacks that had been planned were put on hold, including the mission to rescue the scientists sheltering in a secure underground laboratory at

Fort Deitrich. They were meant to be a priority as they were confident they could manufacture an effective treatment as soon as they got samples of the virus and a means to mass produce it.

He knew the Russians had landed in San Antonio and itched to get involved in the action. He was a member of the elite forces of the United States and the fact that the Russians were running a mission on US soil hurt his professional pride.

"Bear," he said, "remind General Welch I have a unit here ready and waiting to assist in POTUS extraction."

"When they need you I'm sure they'll come a hollering, Troy. But I will forward your request," Gus said to him, his face showing concern. "How are your people holding up?"

"Desperate for some payback, Gus," he answered with a tired sigh, "desperate. Can I request we do a recon mission to the camp at Caldwell? It will give us a more accurate assessment of enemy strength and location in the area. We are better when we are doing something and a few days in the bush will stop them sitting here brooding. If the infection has reached the camps, we need to know. Anything we can give the scientists at Fort Deitrich could help them."

Senator Gus Howard was one of the few senior political figures who was both alive and not under Chinese control. He also had the respect of everyone at the Holly River Base. His position as one of the leaders was not by invite or by asking. The role naturally suited him, and he found himself doing it without realizing.

Gus looked at Troy and smiled.

"Come on, Troy. You know as well as I that you get every communication I do. If you are asking for permission, then it's because you don't expect it to be granted. Whereas if the request is agreed by me then the call comes in and you ain't here, I'm the one General Welch rips a new asshole."

Troy shrugged. "Can't blame a man for trying. Look if we leave now, we know the route is clear almost to the camp. We can be there and back in a day. I think the intel gain will be worth it. It will also be a good opportunity to integrate the various units that have arrived here and for me to see how good they all claim to be."

"So, it's a training mission now?"

"Oh come on, Gus," Troy said, "we just want to do something useful, that's all. My men and I are hurting; we failed to protect the POTUS. The camp mission and the one to Fort Deitrich have been put on hold. We are no use to the country sitting round a campfire stirring a pot of beans. Most of the militia leaders are not due here for a few days, we may as well make ourselves useful and get our finely tuned asses in the fight."

Numbers at the Holly River Base were increasing daily as more followed the cryptic message on posters he had distributed. Bear had contacted some of the militias in Virginia and other states. With the already established contact with General Welch at Cheyenne Mountain, Gus had organized a war council and invited militia leaders to attend with the aim of agreeing how the various units could coordinate their efforts. Most were due to arrive over the next few days.

Gus smiled at the captain. "Let me make a call. Bear, get me General Welch please."

A short while later Gus went to find Troy who was sitting outside around a fire, drinking coffee with his men.

"Captain Gardner. You have thirty-six hours," he said with a smile. "They are working on the logistics to extract the president. Her location is currently the safest place for her to be until the best plan is agreed. You have been authorized to gather intel on the camp and the location of enemy forces in and around the Caldwell area."

Troy nodded his thanks to the senator and stood up and addressed his men, saying simply, "Ten minutes."

He did not need to tell his men what equipment to take. They were superbly trained and would know.

Five minutes later as Troy was going through the route and the alternatives with his sergeants, the men loaded the last of their equipment onto the trucks.

CALDWELL

Toby and Harris stood at the fence with the entire population of the camp.

Uncertainty was rife and wild rumors abound. Panic had spread when one loud voice assured everyone that the Chinese had pulled back as they were about to attack them. Hearing this, people either tried to scale the fence or find a safe place to hide.

Harris stood calmly in the middle of the furor, his hand supporting Toby who was swaying unsteadily on his feet. He was as confused as the rest of the camp, but also knew that no one else had any idea what was going on so did not react to the wild speculation being spread by the lips of terrified individuals.

When the masses had fled from the perimeter of the fence, he led Toby to it. Escaping from the camp seemed the right move to make. The guards would not have left unless there was a good reason and they had deliberately knocked over the water barrel as they departed.

He studied the fence. It was made from twelve-foot-high heavy-duty chain link, topped with a double row of razor wire.

None of the panicking inmates had successfully scaled it, all getting entangled and badly cut by the razor-sharp barbs. With a pair of wire cutters, you could be through it in seconds, but he knew no such tool existed in the camp. He walked up to the gate to inspect it. It was secured by a padlock and a locking bar that had been dropped into place. A lorry would be able to smash through it, but half-starved weakened men would be able to do no more than rattle it.

Eventually an air of defeat and despondency settled over the exhausted hungry and thirsty inmates. Gathering back in the yard most slumped to the ground, all their energy spent. Harris looked at the men. He never chose to stand out from the crowd, preferring the solitary life working the late shift as a security guard at a security firm in Cleveland and spending his off-duty hours in his apartment watching television.

When the attacks happened he eventually let two people into his secured area and, to his surprise, found their company to his liking. They had stuck together when he deemed it safe to leave and he assumed the role as their guide and protector, finding that he was more capable in the role than he had ever thought.

When they were captured by the Chinese and Marissa was separated from them, he continued to protect and look after Toby. Looking at the men in the yard he knew that most had given up and were just waiting for whatever was going to happen next to arrive.

If he could have gotten Toby out of the camp alone he would have, but for the plan he was forming in his mind he needed help from others. Still supporting Toby, he walked to the center of the yard. His physical size made him an imposing figure amongst the ragged malnourished group and eyes were drawn to him. The low murmur of voices subsided into silence.

"We need to get out of this camp. Not one of us knows if the Chinese will come back or what they are planning next, but I think that remaining here will be more dangerous than leaving."

A voice called out, "We can't get out. Don't you think we haven't tried?"

"Yes, but you haven't been working together. We can't break down the gate, it's too strong. The ground is too hard, and the fence dug in too deep to dig under it. If we work together to construct a ladder or platform, we can build something that will enable us to get over the fence."

Another voice: "And then what do we do?"

"Anything is better than staying here, waiting to die. There is no water in here and lack of that will kill us in days. I don't know what is out there, we may get captured again or we may find somewhere safe away from the Chinese. If we stay here, we will definitely die, if we leave we *may* die. I know which option I prefer."

Most of the men in the yard looked at him and nodded. They sat more erect and alert, the veil of despair lifting as the potential of escape and life was realized.

Harris looked at the faces staring at him. "If we all can go and find long lengths of lumber and something to fix them together we can make a start."

One voice called back, a slight lisp adorning the words, "Where are we meant to find those?"

Keeping calm, he replied, "Look around us. There should be plenty of timber we can scavenge, the blankets can be used to tie everything together. Look, I don't really know, we just need to find what we can and do our best."

Galvanized and with purpose most went off to start looking for materials and soon the sounds of banging and splintering wood echoed around the yard. The pile of lumber grew. Harris organized a few who claimed to have practical skills to begin constructing something that would enable them to scale the fence. It was slow work involving a lot of trial and error on how to securely join timber together with what they had available to make it strong enough, but eventually two rough-looking ladders were made.

The camp had united under the common aim to escape, and many willing hands helped lift the first section into place. After a few precarious moments the other section was hauled up and let drop over the high fence to form a ladder down the other side. Blankets were gathered to place over the razor wire.

As soon as it was in place everyone cheered, but then the mood changed. The way out of the camp was open and everyone wanted to be first to escape. Harris, who had climbed up the ladder to test it and place the blankets, turned and saw the crowd that seconds ago had been unified in success, jostling and pushing past each other in their eagerness to be first.

He held his hands out and bellowed, "STOP!"

The advancing crowd paused.

"We don't know what's out there yet or which direction is the safest to go. If you run off in the wrong direction, you could run headlong into the Chinese. Please could we stop and think for a moment."

The crowd, seeing the sense of what he was saying, backed off a few paces as he descended the ladder.

"I suggest a few of us go and check the immediate area out. I don't know the area at all—are there any locals who can volunteer?"

Four stepped forward to volunteer and the rest of the camp lined the fences and watched as they scaled the ladder and ran off to reconnoiter the area.

CHAPTER FIFTEEN

CHEYENNE MOUNTAIN

General Welch sat in his chair at the command center watching the screens displaying live satellite images and plotting the Chinese fleet's course.

The second Chinese wave was approaching the western seaboard of the United States at maximum revolutions. Like an approaching swarm of malevolent monsters, they promised death to their enemies.

An exhausted-looking young lieutenant turned to him. "Sir, that's confirmation. They are splitting and heading for four different ports. ETA between six and eight hours."

Banging his fist hard against the desk he exclaimed, "The *goddamn bastards* will be landing before we can do anything about it! Dammit, get me O'Reilly on the line."

Seven of the nine carrier battle groups in the US fleet had

been in their home ports when the Chinese attacked. The ports had not been targeted by the nuclear weapons, but by the new and unknown weapon the Chinese had unleashed from their carrier-launched stealth bombers.

Despite going on full alert the moment the first inbound missiles were detected, the new weapon, designed with the utmost secrecy by the Chinese, was impossible for the many layers of defense that a carrier group could throw up around itself to detect or counter.

The bombs had fallen from the sky unnoticed until the first detonation which heralded the arrival of a barrage of high explosives seemingly coming from nowhere. The first wave neutralized any offensive capability of these fleets, which for so long had been the most powerful force projector on the planet. They had the capability to sail anywhere and instantly be the most dominant force in the neighborhood, bringing either peace or annihilation depending on whose side you were on. The mere arrival of a United States carrier battle group had the ability to diffuse potential trouble spots quickly.

Now, as the second and third waves of bombs fell, all that was left of the once proud and mighty symbols of a global power were the burnt, twisted remains of their hulls. Only two carrier groups survived: The USS Theodore Roosevelt was in the Persian Gulf and the USS Ronald Reagan was in it the Southern Pacific partaking in a joint maritime training exercise with the combined

Australian and New Zealand navies.

With the reports of unknown weapons destroying ships at anchor in their home ports, the mood on the remaining flotillas was dark. General Welch had, on day one of the attacks, been fearful the remaining ships at sea could become targets, and had ordered all the ships of the Pacific fleet to head to a friendly foreign port, and the ships in the Persian Gulf to 'get the hell out of there' and make best speed to the South Atlantic.

The only vessels he remained deployed were the submarines. About half were in a home port at the time of the attack and so shared the same fate as the surface vessels, but the others were still out there, silently cruising through the ocean's depths, awaiting orders.

Admiral Jim O'Reilly had assumed command of the Pacific fleet following the destruction of the base at Pearl Harbor. Transferring his flag to the USS Ronald Reagan, he had spent the time gathering and marshalling the forces at his disposal ready for the order to strike back to be given.

The Ohio ballistic missile submarines, or 'Boomers' as they were referred to by most in the navy, he positioned in a line across the Pacific Ocean ready at a single command to unleash their cargoes of either nuclear or conventional destruction. Every fast attack submarine available was either patrolling the Atlantic, trying to track the unknown number of very stealthy Chinese submarines that had launched nuclear missiles at the US, or were shadowing the huge fleet of Chinese vessels that was now hours away from the West Coast.

General Welch had the call set on speaker. "Jim, it's Doug," he said, the tiredness making his voice heavy. "Report."

"Every vessel we have is at the highest level of alert. Just give me the command and I can fill the seas with Ticonderoga-class Cruisers and destroyers and thousands of pissed off sailors," he declared vehemently. "The subs are tracking the Chinese fleet, but the net they have thrown around themselves is large and tight. If we start poking them, I fear we will lose some subs for no gain."

"There is nothing we can do to stop them landing, I agree," Welch said, "but how soon can you get some of your ships in strike range?"

"The subs are already there. In eighteen hours I can have ten destroyers past the date line and in theatre. The carrier group at best speed is five days out."

"Jim, the Russians and Canadians are closer. I'm authorizing you to open up channels of communication and get a workable plan of attack together. Report back ASAP."

"Yes, sir. I am also getting the intelligence about another build-up of troops in Chinese and Korean ports. Do I need to consider the option of a third invasion fleet setting sail?"

Welch sighed again. "It looks that way. They are not being as secretive about this and as you can tell they seem to be stripping the cupboards bare on transport. Agents in country are reporting cruise liners being commandeered for troops. We are trying to figure out what naval assets they have left to protect this fleet. Therefore, I want you to plan an attack on the second invasion fleet. It will tie up any Chinese forces and stop them being redeployed to protect the third wave." He paused, not wanting his next words to sound trite.

"They have hit us hard and we are in a world of hurt, but now we have the president back we can start looking at our offensive options. The Brits are back on side and are assisting in getting our European-based troops home." Welch chuckled mirthlessly. "Well, to Canada at least. I am awaiting confirmation from them of what military resources they can also offer. The board is set, and the pieces are starting to drop into place. If we can get the next phase right, we can go from our current defensive posture and begin the containment stage."

"That's great news, sir. I think that at this stage my people will be more interested in blowing them back to hell. Tell me," he said changing the subject, "how is life at the mountain now?"

"Better now I can go outside for some fresh air, thanks. The Russians have landed in force and have set up a strong perimeter. I don't think the Chinese will be back any time soon. It's a strange world we are living in, Jim. We are accommodating our new allies in the complex itself as well as outside. I'm getting used to the sight of the Russians poking about making themselves at home, while a part of me is wondering what the hell they are doing and if they are planting bugs or other clever things their intel guys can come up with."

The admiral laughed again. "We'd be doing the same, I'm sure. Anyway, I'll be back as soon as I get a plan together with the Canadians and Russians. O'Reilly out."

PACIFIC OCEAN, 200 MILES WEST OF SAN DIEGO

Captain Wayne Grant was perturbed. In the first few days following the bombardment and subsequent invasion, all the news had been positive. The initial goals had been achieved and ground forces were spreading throughout the country, taking control of vast areas and the citizens they contained. Any surviving military assets were seized and placed under Chinese control.

He had anticipated an American counter attack and whilst most celebrated the lack of one, he could not understand why no attempt had been made to stop them so far. His Chinese masters were boasting that the American devil had been utterly defeated. When he had tried to instill caution, stating that most of the Pacific fleet was out there and untouched, he was ridiculed and shouted down. He was reminded that he wasn't one of them, at least by the bravest of the Chinese officers, and he bit his tongue so as not to hit them with too much truth that they didn't want to hear.

They wanted his insight on the American mind, that much was clear, and had listened and learned from what he had told them over the years, but now the sight of the impending victory clouded their judgment. He believed that their arrogance blinded them.

As far as they were concerned the country was leaderless, the president had been captured, caught hiding away in a bunker. The country would soon surrender and become a satellite of China. They could not comprehend that others would, without orders from the highest level, continue the fight. They thought that the missing Pacific fleet was in hiding and when the surrender was broadcast, would meekly return and bow to their new masters.

He gazed ahead as the ship ploughed through the undulating seas, heading toward a country he once called home, but now where he would be called a traitor.

CHAPTER SIXTEEN

COBRA, DOWNING STREET, LONDON

Adriene Winslet sat waiting for her cabinet members and heads of the armed forces to file into the office and take their seats.

"Good morning, everyone. Before we turn our eyes further afield can we have an update on the domestic situation."

The minister in charge of food and agriculture spoke first: "The news is more positive. The price gouging has stopped following the emergency laws we passed, and the distribution situation has calmed down. Food manufacturers are increasing production to make up for some of the shortfall in imports and we are working with them to maintain the supply chain.

"The 'ugly vegetable-in-law', as the media are calling it, that we passed is having an immediate impact. Thousands of tons of extra fruit and vegetables that would otherwise have been thrown away are supplementing what we used to import.

"The media are now working with us to educate people on planting, harvesting, and eking out what food people have." He stopped and looked around the table. "I know the phrase 'dig for victory' seems to have caught the media's attention, but the public seem to be embracing it too."

A tabloid paper had reprinted a Second World War poster encouraging all citizens to do their bit and dig over any suitable space to plant vegetables.

"Reports are coming in of a nationwide seed shortage. Within hour of the media picking up on the story, every shop that sold seeds ran out. We are working with suppliers and distributors to set up seed distribution centers around the country to keep up with the demand—"

Adriene interrupted him. "Yes, that's all well and good," she said peevishly, "I'm certainly no expert, but seeds take some time before they turn into a carrots and cabbages, do they not? What is the situation regarding feeding the country until then?"

"I believe that if we keep on as we are doing then most of the shortfall will be met by education on food preparation and economical use. Also the reductions in wastage all the way through from manufacture to end user we are implementing will have a dramatic increase on the volume reaching the shelves. The nation has really got behind this now they understand the situation is none of our doing. The change has been remarkable."

She turned to head of the police force. "Is it as calm out there as reports are suggesting?"

"Yes, ma'am. The majority of rioting, as I reported earlier, stopped as soon as your speech was broadcast. There are obviously still pockets of lawlessness out there as a minority are taking the opportunity to 'shop' for new television sets and the like, but it's under control. It remains quiet on the whole, and reported crime is down dramatically. Don't get me wrong, the career criminals are still out there doing what they do, but people seem to be too busy with the 'dig for victory' idea that they are all too preoccupied to cause trouble."

She nodded and turned to her foreign minister with a smile. "So, tell me how our European cousins are faring?"

"The situation in Europe changed overnight when Russia stopped exporting oil and natural gas following their announcement that all production is being diverted for internal use now the country is on a war footing. Food riots are spreading as the promised imports from America have not materialized and the situation will not be helped when the refineries run out of crude, which will not be too long away. France especially is anticipating widespread unrest."

Adriene saw the opportunity she was waiting for to drop the bombshell. "And what is the situation regarding our own oil and gas imports?"

The foreign secretary looked at the prime minister who nodded her consent for him to continue. "As of this morning we have agreed an import deal for Russian oil and gas. The tankers are diverting from their existing courses as we speak." He fidgeted with his tie before continuing. "Apparently, the ban on exports they imposed does not include allies of Russia."

"And what else does Russia export?" she asked.

He smiled again. "Russia, in recent years, has turned its food industry around to stop its reliance on imports and only two years ago changed from being a net importer of certain products to a net exporter. I can also happily inform the cabinet that at the same time we signed the energy deal we signed a deal to import grain, fish, sugar, and other products from Russia. From what I understand, any shortfall we may have been anticipating will be negated by these new imports."

The room burst into noise as most around the table demanded more details.

Adriene waited for the noise to subside before she continued. "The country may run out of avocadoes and cucumbers, but with a little adjustment to what we are used to finding on the supermarket shelves and the efforts of our own people, the country's food worries are over for now. Now, General, please inform the cabinet of how your plans are progressing."

The general stood to address the room. "The withdrawal of most of our soldiers deployed overseas is progressing. In certain areas we know this will have a destabilizing effect which will be exacerbated as other countries are following suit and recalling their soldiers back to their own domestic bases. There is, unfortunately, little we can do about this. Our own defense and security must take priority." He paused to clear his throat. "Following a conference between the United States, Russia, Canada, and ourselves a way forward has been agreed." He glanced around the room for questions before he continued with their naval dispositions.

"A Royal Navy task force consisting of the carrier HMS Queen Elizabeth, frigates, destroyers, and submarines is currently being assembled and will shortly depart for the east coast of the United States where, with the Royal Canadian Navy and the Russian Black Sea fleet, and some surviving United States ships and submarines, a blockade of the entire east coast of America will begin. We have prioritized returning United States soldiers to Canada first. Then we will be deploying two guard regiments to fall under the command of a joint multination force."

"And what of our special forces, General?" asked an aide to the prime minister, eager to get his voice heard.

General Lloyd regarded the young man coldly but kept his opinions to himself. "Two squadrons of SAS have already been dispatched following a request from General Welch. They lost most of their special forces when Fort Bragg was destroyed in the initial attack. They have a list of high-value targets that need rescuing or locating. I am reluctant to commit more at this point as I consider the situation in Europe to be highly unstable and until a clearer picture emerges, I feel it prudent to have the capability to protect our borders. Another Chinese invasion force is approaching the west coast. There is little that can be done to stop it currently, but I believe some harassing action is being planned whilst the combined forces of the US and Russian Pacific fleets move into position to close the door on the west coast. Once both blocking forces are in place there still will be approximately half a million Chinese troops on American soil."

He shuffled papers to find the next piece of relevant intelligence. "The situation still hangs on a knife edge. The Chinese have destroyed or captured most major US military bases and resources. With the numbers of troops they have on the ground, they represent a formidable force. If I can give you a comparison: On D-Day, the allies landed one hundred and fifty-six thousand soldiers and that was to liberate the whole of Europe. We will not have near that number and the United States is by far a bigger land mass. The challenge we are facing is daunting."

The prime minister asked the general, "Do we feel the situation in Europe will become a threat to us?"

"We are monitoring it carefully," General Lloyd answered with a politician's skill. "In all honesty we do not know what will happen. But if we look at the facts, there are many independent nations with a combined population of over six hundred million. All who are currently experiencing food, and most likely very soon, energy shortages. I imagine their individual governments are having similar discussions that we have had and are probably coming up with similar solutions. What they will not have is an answer to how to fill the gaping holes that have appeared in their supply chain. I will leave the politics up to you, Prime Minister, but as history shows time and time again, desperate nations perform desperate acts. Also, the population within Europe can be highly mobile as there are no border restrictions. Mass migration is a real possibility as people move to wherever they think has more food."

He paused again, conscious that he was dominating the floor, but no interruptions came. "There are many hypothetical scenarios we can discuss and plan for. One we need to consider, and I would recommend be implemented, is to close all borders immediately. When the rest of Europe discovers we have what they do not, it does not take a lot of imagination to know where people will be heading. We can barely feed ourselves, but we *cannot* allow our domestic situation to deteriorate again due to potentially millions more wanting what we have." He let those words hang as he was effectively recommending that their island nation to go into a full economic lockdown.

"From a military point of view, the armed forces will be essential in the task to close and protect our borders. There will be the real possibility of confrontations with other European armed forces as we fulfil our duty. The rules of engagement need to be decided and decided quickly."

The room remained silent when he had finished. In one meeting they had gone from the elation that the nation's food and energy supply situation was now looking more positive, to the real threat that they could be facing armed conflict with their European neighbors.

Adriene spoke: "Ladies and gentlemen, we need the country behind the tough decisions we may have to make in the future. We must take this to Parliament. Are we in agreement with General Lloyd's proposal to seal our borders? Might I remind you all that Europe as a whole has decided to sit this out rather than confront Chinese aggression."

She shrugged and nodded in the direction of General Lloyd. "We almost did the same too before reason prevailed. We must remember, though, that they are not our enemy. They chose to stay neutral. Unfortunately for them the consequences of that decision are not yet fully clear, but the consequences of us potentially being deluged with innumerable refugees from hunger and public disorder are clear. We must put the country and its population first."

She asked for a show of hands which unanimously agreed to the plan. "Thank you. Now please go and get Parliament on board with the proposals. As soon as we adjourn I will call the leader of the opposition to fully appraise him. Support from across the floor will be essential if we want this to go smoothly."

CHAPTER SEVENTEEN

The Reverend Jackson Charles Harris smiled at Cal. "This, son, is your lucky day. We are in regular contact with Captain Gardner and others from the Holly River Base. The militias are gathering under the one banner now: The Old Glory. It's why we are here. We are making our way up from Kentucky to Holly River for a war council with him and other militia leaders. He requested we scout the eastern approach to the Appalachians on our way. We spotted your bus bearing Chinese markings behind us on the road and decided to start the campaign early. The plan is to block any access to the mountains, so we can use them as our springboard to free the eastern states." His words wavered, the fingers of his right hand flickering over the worn edges of the bible in his pocket that went everywhere with him.

"It's going to be a long road, but we are building our strength and resources, biding our time until we can drive those goddamn commie bastards out of our home and straight back to hell."

He looked again at the other passengers on the bus. "I'm not hearing any accents from around this neck of the woods. Where are y'all from?"

"Gordon, myself, and a few others are from the UK," Cal explained. "The rest are from other European countries. The Chinese had negotiated our release and were sending us to a ship at Norfolk, I think, to get us all home. That was until the cruise missiles started flying overhead. I don't think we will be going anytime soon now. As I said before, I persuaded the others to stick with me and to try and get to Captain Gardner. I suppose now the best way for me to get home is to offer whatever help I can." He swallowed, forcing back down the emotions that threatened to push back out into the open. "Someone who I was...close to...died from radiation poisoning and the more I dwell on it the more I want to make them pay."

He indicated to Gordon who was beside him. "That's why I stopped the bus. Gordon and I just discovered we served in the same brigade in the Royal Marines. You saw us doing a bit of bonding. Bloody glad we did now as you were about to open fire on us."

"Are you two prepared to fight to help free us?" the reverend asked pointedly.

Gordon leaned forward. "Reverend, if you'll take an old soldier who bears a few scars and the creaking joints to prove it, I'll be happy to offer whatever help I can. I must tell you though, I am a distantly related to Lord Cornwallis and you colonials gave him a right drubbing at Yorktown. I hope I can make up for it by being on the right side this time."

Jackson bellowed with laughter. "We would be happy to have you despite your family's military history. If you can forgive us colonials," he added sarcastically. "Kentucky and Virginia have a proud record for fighting for their independence. We haven't got the French helping us this time though, and if we are going to win this latest war for independence, we are going to need every volunteer we can get."

He looked at the sky which was darkening as night began to fall. "We were scouting for a place to camp when we spotted you heading our way. You would be welcome to join us. We can travel in convoy to Holly River in the morning."

Cal looked at Gordon, who nodded in agreement. "Thank you, we would appreciate that. We are getting low on fuel, I don't suppose you have a few gallons spare?"

"Sure, we can give you a few gallons of gas, do you have enough for a few more miles?"

Cal looked at the gauge on the dashboard. "Yes, we should be fine. But I think this thing runs on diesel not LPG."

Gordon started laughing. "Cal, remember where we are. The Americans, since they shrugged off the cloak of English rule, have spent the last few hundred years destroying the Queen's English, the language we blessed them with. Every time I come to the

States I do try to re-educate them, but I feel that it has been left too late and they are condemned forever to speak what they proudly call 'Merican English. It does make me shudder at times dear boy."

The reverend started laughing. His deep booming laugh filled the air. "I think we'll all get along just fine."

He turned and spoke to one of his men who approached him. "My men have scouted a campsite set way off the road which will make a safe camp for tonight. If you would like to follow us there we can get properly acquainted. Do you mind if I travel with you, so we can continue talking?"

Cal looked for and pulled the lever that opened the door saying, "Not at all. Hop on board."

Cal put the bus into gear and followed the pickups and ATVs of the militia. Jackson, as he told both Cal and Gordon to call him, shook their hands when entering the bus, then stood next to Gordon as Cal drove.

He answered their questions about the militia he commanded. The church he led was the core. In the foothills of the Kentucky mountains his congregation had, for generations, loyally served their God and country. The militia believed that one day they would need to rise up against a tyrannical government and so vehemently defended their right to bear arms.

When he left the army and turned to God, the militia grew and prospered as more followers joined his church. His sermons about the degradation and destruction of the American way of life struck a chord with many who flocked to hear him speak. Cal's understanding of militias from TV programs were that they were all far-right fanatics with compounds and stockpiles of guns, ammunition, and food who resisted any interference to their way or life. He asked if his militia was similar.

"There are some groups like that out there for sure, but we are a law-abiding community centered around our church. Most who live in the community go to church and are considered part of the militia. We do not divide ourselves between gender and age, if you want to serve and are old enough to hold a gun then we welcome you.

"We run regular training camps and exercises, but they are more community events, attended and enjoyed by all. I am their spiritual leader, but I also look after their physical well-being. The drills we run are based on good old-fashioned boot camp training, military tactics and strategies. Yes, they all moan and gripe about them, but when I stand there and look at my congregation and see none looking dangerously overweight, I know I am looking after my people the best I can. Stockpiles of weapons are not necessary. Every member of the community enjoys the rights given to them under the constitution and own many firearms and the ammunition needed to use them.

"When the bombs started falling and paratroopers invaded our land, I called the militia together." His voice shook with pride and emotion. "Within one hour, one hundred percent of the militia presented themselves for duty outside the doors of my church. Seeing them arranged into their platoons coming to attention when I stepped outside was one of the proudest moments of my life."

Following the vehicles in front, Cal turned off the road and slowed down as the bus bumped along the rutted trail that weaved through the trees. Eventually, the trail opened out to a cleared area of forest, a sign displaying the rules of the campsite indicating they had arrived.

CHAPTER
EIGHTEEN

Sitting in front of the radio, Madeline was talking to General Welch. "I appreciate your concerns, General, but I will not leave the country and hide across the border. What message will that give to the American people if the first thing I do is to run away?"

"Madam President, your safety is of the utmost concern. We cannot risk you falling into enemy hands again."

"General, I agree," she said emphatically. "Currently I am being protected by hundreds of armed Americans and a brigade of Russian paratroopers. I am safe enough for now. General Liu on the other hand needs to be moved to somewhere where he can be of greater assistance to us. He is a proud man who feels his country is being betrayed by its leadership. If we handle it right, I believe he could play a key role in changing the regime and ending this before it's too late."

"Too late, Madam President? We are already at war and fighting for our very existence. I am not sure how much worse it can get."

"General, the world is watching and waiting. How much longer before other countries start to look toward a weaker neighbor now that the United States is not able to fulfil its role as the world's policeman? We are at war, but we must try to stop this escalating, because if it does, I fear the world will be on the brink."

"I understand. The planning with the Russians, British, and Canadians is almost complete. Can I at least recommend we recover you to Cheyenne Mountain? You will be secure here and it will be easier for you to communicate and oversee the operations."

"General, I am no military leader; you are. It is your job to formulate and propose your plans to me for approval. I do not need to be sitting at your side to do that. Find me somewhere where I can do my job and help rally and lead the American people to victory. And as for communication, are you telling me we do not have the means for me to talk to someone from anywhere on the planet? General, find me a place and the equipment and get back to me with your recommendations."

Putting the receiver down she turned to Sebastian. "What do you suggest we do?"

"Madam President, as I have already told you, we are not sure how effective our radio encryption is. We have intelligence to suggest the Chinese can break in and track our comms. We need to move now and return to base."

For security, a remote broadcasting location had been set up at another property ten miles from the ranch deep in the Texas countryside. Madeline had been escorted there by Sebastian and a strong contingent of both Russian paratroopers and American militia members. "Sebastian, that is not what I meant."

"Madam President, I know. But for now, my primary concern is your safety so if we could please get moving."

Outside, the hundreds of Russians and Americans who had accompanied her as her personal guard boarded the fleet of SUVs and pickup trucks and, with Madeline in the center vehicle, the convoy sped back to the ranch. Thirty seconds after leaving the property the driver without warning swerved the car off the road and shouted. Sebastian without thinking threw himself across the president, shielding her body with his, and screamed at the driver to keep going.

The boom of an explosion washed over the car now hurtling down the road. Sebastian uncovered the president from the footwell and helped her back to the seat. She looked through the back window at a house which was now burning fiercely.

"It's as I feared, Madam President. That missile locked in on the radio signal we were emitting; we are going to have to be more inventive on how we communicate from now on. The Chinese are far from defeated."

Shocked from the near miss, Madeline sat thinking before

she spoke. "Or we find and destroy wherever the missile was launched from. If every time we turn on a radio we fear a missile, then this burgeoning movement will fail. Without communication and coordination, we will just be small groups fighting locally and individually until our numbers are so eroded by the Chinese we will become ineffective. The only route to beating them is coordinating a national offensive and striking them where it hurts. That way we will wear away their capabilities until the balance swings on our favor."

Sebastian looked at the president. "Madam President," he said with deep respect, "I just heard you tell the general you are no military leader. You were wrong. I agree, this threat is new, and we must counter it immediately."

They were both correct. The Chinese were beginning to deploy their latest Direction-Finding Counter Insurgency missile batteries around the country. These small, vehicle-portable weapons were another asset they had developed in secret away from the world's view.

Completely automated and independent, each battery, once in location, needed no human input other than to be protected by squads of soldiers who would reload it once its original complement of small hypersonic short-range missiles was depleted.

Its advanced computer system was overseen by operatives in Beijing. A network of small satellites launched into orbit under the guise of commercial communication and navigation units looked down over the United States. Each region where they were deployed had a relay station which linked all the launchers into the main system.

Capable of intercepting all radio and telecommunication signals, its programming interpreted and deciphered each intercept, deciding in milliseconds if it posed a threat. It was currently set to intercept and identify all signals, but to only treat those that were encrypted or short burst as a target of interest.

Ham radio operators all over the country were communicating with each other; they were the backbone of the resistances' means of communication. These conversations were being recorded and sent to analysts to interpret and use the intelligence gained to help the efforts to destroy all threats to the Chinese mission of conquest. At the stroke of a key, missiles would rain down on their locations.

The one drawback of this highly advanced system was that its portability meant the missiles were small and limited to a twenty-mile range. Its warhead, although powerful, was capable of only limited destruction.

The missile batteries were intended for the second phase of the invasion; to be used to stop the threat of organized counter insurgency. Madeline had unfortunately been within the range of one of the first units set up in Texas. The battery that fired the missile had only just been activated after driving to a location twenty miles from San Antonio. If fate had allowed the battery to be operational ten minutes earlier, it would have received the signal and launched its missile whilst she was talking to General Welch. Luckily for her, it only received the targeting coordinates when it became active just after she ended the transmission.

Hundreds of these systems, designed and built solely for the American operation, were currently being unloaded from transport planes to be mounted on adapted requisitioned pickup trucks. Soon they would be deployed in an ever-growing umbrella around the country.

Madeline strode into the large central room of the ranch that had become the headquarters of the Texas resistance. General Liu was sitting on a chair around the large table. Sergeant Tommy Cho was by his side acting as his aide-cum-bodyguard-cum-prison guard. Sebastian went up to the radio set they had been using to communicate with other cells and to the surprise of its operator turned it off, telling her to leave it alone and to stop broadcasting.

He then sat at another desk and put on some headphones attached to some very old-looking equipment and, after twisting a few dials to adjust the frequency, began tapping at a Morse code key. After a few minutes he stood up, removed the headphones, and approached Madeline.

"Madam President, I have just sent a Morse code message about this new missile threat to be relayed to General Welch

136

advising him to tell all he can about the dangers of radio communication."

Madeline looked alarmed. "Madam President, please do not worry. I can guarantee that the last thing the Chinese will be monitoring is low frequency, single bandwidth AM signals."

Not fully understanding what he had said, she nodded and turned to the Chinese general. "General, I have just escaped death by seconds. You have deployed, and I do not know the correct terminology, missiles that target radio transmissions. You must tell us what you know about these systems now."

The general leaned forward over the table and bowed his head. "Madam President, you place me in an awkward position. I am Chinese and love my country. You cannot expect me to betray my knowledge of the weapons we have developed to beat you."

He paused. "But I also know the capabilities of these weapons. How do you say? They could be a game changer and severely hamper your efforts at resistance. Any information I give will undoubtedly cost the lives of my own countrymen, but I must weigh that against the costs of not assisting you and stopping the madness that has fallen upon us all."

Madeline sat next to him and placed her hand on his arm. "General, believe me I do understand, but the country is crippled. As you know, your strikes destroyed our ability to communicate effectively. Without the radios we will not be able to communicate and get to a position where we can stop this. We need your help, sir."

The general sat staring at Madeline. From the little contact they had had together his respect for her was growing. She was completely different to the leaders he had followed his entire life. They were God-like creatures whose power and authority were not to be questioned. To utter one word against them was placing your very life at risk.

His position brought him into contact with some of them. They were untouchable, not interested in other views or opinions, only that you would do what they commanded. They scoffed at Western leaders and their weaknesses at having to obey the will of the people. Changing policy if public opinion went against them. The Chinese leaders did not care what the public thought. They were only there to serve the country, and they were the country. Madeline Tanner was comparatively unknown to him before the invasion. He knew she was third in line to succeed in the Presidency and the file he had received on her held little more than a picture and a brief description of her political career.

He had met her in San Antonio when she had been captured. The cowed and beaten image she portrayed did little to change his opinion given in the report that she was weak and would easily be manipulated if captured. Now he had seen her covered in blood from the wounded Russian soldier she had helped; she had overpowered Fen Shu, knocking her out with a single punch and then persuaded her guards to flee; she'd changed from captive to captor when she tied her up until the Russians had reached them.

The respect she received naturally from the Americans had turned to admiration when the stories the Russians told them spread. An internal conflict had been raging inside him since Sebastian had refused to accept his surrender. He had sat outwardly calm not showing his emotions whilst his brain had been racing as he wrestled between his sense of duty, his conscience, and in no small part his own ambitions.

He knew that China's mission to conquer America was most likely now doomed to fail. The Chinese had already poured hundreds of thousands of their best soldiers and vast stores of equipment into the country and more was on the way. The fight would be long, hard and bitter, but he now understood they had underestimated the American people and completely miscalculated the international response.

If the world had left America to its fate, then they would have probably succeeded. He would have used a gentler approach to bring the American citizens to accept the reality that they had new masters. His leaders had chosen the more brutal route—one they understood—of creating camps and forcing citizens to work as slave labor leaving only those who provided the goods or services they needed free, albeit closely controlled and monitored through a network of spies and informants.

They had anticipated the Canadian reaction, but their military, even though it was well trained and equipped was relatively small and would not pose a threat. They had planned to mollify them with advantageous trade agreements and offers of multibillion-dollar infrastructure investments, relying on the greed of the government to curb any aggression they might consider.

Learning the Russians had joined the fight shocked him. All the advisors and intelligence reliably informed them they would sit aside and watch as their great enemy fell. They would most likely use it to their advantage and reassume control of some of the countries and territories that they had lost when the Soviet Union fell apart, and the world's eyes were elsewhere.

And without America to intervene what could anyone do about it?

These experts and advisors, though, trying to garner favor with their masters, only chose the options that they thought they wanted to hear. The Russian military had long been in decline and considered a shell of its former self. Its southern border with China, once a solid wall of bunkers and fortifications was now reduced to a few outposts staffed by bored, under-trained and under-equipped soldiers who considered the posting more of a punishment than duty.

The rejuvenation of their military in recent years was watched with interest, but once again all advice reliably informed the country's leaders that it was to counter American control spreading east from Europe and that they would never have the courage to limit China's own expansion plans. China thought that as their financial stranglehold on the world grew, no nation would have the courage to harm the hand that feeds it.

The British were known to be a stubborn and proud people, but again China had invested heavily in the country and believed the control they could exert would force them not to get involved. Without the imports they controlled both directly and indirectly, the country would fall. Their military was one of the best trained in the world and though small, should never be underestimated.

Every country in the world modelled their special forces on the SAS and even though they only numbered in their hundreds, the psychological effect on their enemies thinking they were out there, waiting to strike, made them equivalent to a force many times larger.

General Liu reached a decision. He held Madeline's gaze. "I will help you," he said. "If only to save my country from being destroyed. For my own benefit, could records be kept proving to my own countrymen that I chose to help not because I am a traitor, but because I love my country and want to save it? If one day I can return I need to hold my head up and not bowed in shame."

"You have my word, General."

He nodded his thanks and patted her hand that still lay on his arm.

"Mister Sebastian? Please get me a map and I will show you where the missile command center is located. All our headquarters are set up on the same principals so the others around the country will be the same.

As Sebastian turned away, Madeline said, "Also, you need to question Fen Shu about where the cure is for the virus. We need that if we are to replicate and mass produce it."

He smiled. "Am I permitted to use enhanced interrogation techniques?"

"As far as I am concerned," she said, suspecting that the generic-sounding term hid a whole raft of atrocities under its skirt, "you can do what the hell you like to the bitch. She is responsible for the deaths of millions of Americans."

"Do not worry, Madam President. I will get her to talk even if it's with her last breath."

"Do not kill her please, Sebastian," interrupted General Liu.

"General, I will do whatever it takes to get her to talk," Sebastian replied sharply. "If she dies, then with all due respect it's none of your business, sir. We need that information."

"But you do not understand…" Liu said hesitantly. "Her uncle is the Chinese President."

Chapter
Nineteen

Gander Airport, Newfoundland, Canada

Gander Airport was once a hive of activity. Now, it was quiet and mostly forgotten. It found fame as an intercontinental flight refueling stop, but that was curtailed by new technology which allowed planes to fly nonstop halfway around the world without the need to refuel.

Maintained as an emergency landing airport for transatlantic flights, its long runways and large aprons had far greater capacity than its current regional airport role.

Its aprons were now full of airplanes that continually landed and took off in a well-choreographed display. Military and civilian passenger planes disgorged the thousands of United States troops repatriated from bases around the world who then waited in the terminal buildings or hangers for orders to arrive.

These men and women were angry. They had been in a

foreign land when the Chinese had attacked. They'd watched the devastation of the nuclear attacks and conventional bombings on televisions mounted on walls of barracks from a country they had left home to help defend and protect. Most knew they had lost family members and friends, and they wanted revenge.

They were continually told by Americans hurriedly dispatched from embassies and consulates across Canada the fight was not over and every one of them would be needed in the coming battles to repel the invaders, and to be patient as the plans were being drawn up. Gander had been selected as it had the capacity to deal with the numbers and its remote location would hopefully keep the activities away from Chinese eyes. Not taking any chances Canadian police and the intelligence service detained any Chinese national or Chinese-Canadian citizen in the surrounding area. Human rights considerations were put on hold as national security took precedence over the feelings of the few involved.

Once again, the ordinary citizens of Gander stepped forward to help, just like they had during the 9-11 terrorist crisis when thousands of passengers were stranded at the airport due to American airspace being shut down and their planes being forced to divert there. Then, as now, they welcomed the unexpected arrivals with open arms and friendliness.

Rallying together they set up soup kitchens to help feed the thousands of soldiers, and distributed blankets and bedding to offer the soldiers some comfort. The Canadian government was sending everything it could to help, but the efforts of the local population augmented this and greatly relieved the pressure on their personnel trying to deal with such a large influx.

In an isolated corner of the airfield a small arrangement of green tents went mostly unnoticed, subtly guarded by soldiers from the Canadian air force base also located at the airport. Lieutenant General Andrew Michaels, commander of the British Special Air Service Regiment, walked into the largest tent occupied by the majors and captains that commanded the troops.

"Chaps, the Yanks have a job for us."

The gathered men quietened down and listened attentively.

"The damn Chinese have released a virus that is killing thousands. Possibly millions. Details are sketchy, but there are some scientists trapped in a bunker at"—he glanced down at his notebook for the place—"Fort Dietrich, who were working on what they reckon is a similar virus. They believe that they can manufacture a cure if they can get hold of some samples of the virus itself."

General Michaels held up his hands. "Before you ask, I do not understand the science or the reason why scientists in other labs can't do this. It is speed that is of the essence. If we can get those people out, along with their research stuff and little test tubes or whatever they keep it in, it will be the quickest way for the cure to be manufactured, saving months of work and millions of lives."

He gave a wry chuckle. "Now that is the easy bit. The

problem is the base was heavily bombed in the initial stages of the attack. Their lab is in a deep underground bunker, so they were safe, but satellite images show the facility was badly damaged. The scientists report the doors are jammed, but as the they are on the wrong side of them, they cannot tell what is causing it. And to complicate matters further the area has a strong enemy presence." He paused for a muted and sarcastic cheer to die down. "Therefore, I am committing both squadrons to the mission. We must insert into a facility deep within enemy territory, most likely dig around to find the entrance. And then extract the fifteen men and women and get them back to a safe country." He looked at the assembled faces, knowing his elite well enough that he expected to see no fear.

"Oh," he added, "and the mission will take place under strict radio silence. We have received a disturbing report about an unknown Chinese anti-radio missile that almost killed the president." He looked at the men facing him. "What's that I hear? A piece of cake, I hear you all cry."

He waited for the polite chuckles to subside. "All the intel we have is on the table. Shall we get on with it, gents?"

The SAS planned their missions collectively as was their tradition. Rank, and especially the divide between the officer classes and the non-commissioned ranks, held no sway in planning; only experience counted. To pass selection and be badged a member of the elite force, you were already the best the British Army had.

The subsequent specialist training in all fields they received gave them unique skills, giving every member the right to take part in planning missions. Ironically, they called this process a 'Chinese Parliament.'

Two hours later the captains, majors and sergeants, the NCOs who were the backbone of the regiment, gathered in the command tent. Lieutenant General Andrew Michaels started the meeting.

"Ginge, you are the senior officer, therefore will be in overall command so can you be the conduit for the meeting please. I know that's unusual, but I can't remember a time so many of us have been involved in one single mission. As the saying goes 'we need to keep this simple, stupid.'"

Ginge, or Major Benjamin Bowden was on his second tour with the SAS. Most officers only serve a single two to three-year stint before returning to their original regiment or a staff job, and only the best of that crop were ever invited back again.

Major Bowden had completed his first secondment to the regiment as a captain, earning the respect and liking of everyone at the base through his leadership, bravery in action, and basic demeanor. When he reluctantly returned to his original regiment he soon achieved the rank of major and performed outstandingly. By his own admission he missed the regiment and all that it stood for. After a few conversations he reapplied and without hesitation, at the first opportunity, they welcomed him back to command A squadron.

The nickname Ginge had been unsurprisingly bestowed upon him due to his bright red hair as soon as he stepped through the regiment's door.

The gap between ordinary ranks and officers was treated differently in the SAS in all matters; not just that of mission planning. Nicknames were common, as in every part of the army, but in the regiment, it was common for these nicknames to be used between the ranks. So even though he was now a major in command of one of the four SAS squadrons, everyone still referred to him as Ginge.

"Thank you, sir," he began. "We propose a HAHO insertion." As the general did before him, he paused for the low cheer at the dangerous and ultimately exciting method of insertion. High altitude high opening required jumping out at an altitude requiring oxygen and popping their canopies to descend slowly with over an hour spent in the freezing sky. That way, there was no loud crack of a parachute deploying at low altitude. "Confirmation of what the Canadians can offer us in the way of transport should be here soon. Confidence is high that the two squadrons can secure the facility and begin the recovery operation. The blast bunnies," he said with a smirk, referring to explosive ordnance specialists, "are also confident they can clear a route through whatever debris may be in the way. The issue we see is maintaining the perimeter we create if the Chinese forces are as strong as intel suggests in the area. A US Ranger battalion is currently in a hanger over the apron kicking their heels and chomping at the bit for some action. I had a quick chat with their CO and they are up for a bit of fun. Can I recommend you formally request for them to be seconded to us for the duration of the mission?"

General Michaels nodded his agreement.

"They have their own transport," Ginge went on, "and now that the bulk of their personnel are this side of the pond the transports are starting to bring rotary wing assets and other goodies which could help us a lot. The extraction phase will begin immediately the targets are located. Fuel range is the issue though, as the facility is beyond the range of most rotary wings without refueling. Our initial thoughts are to extract the targets to an FOB," he explained, not needing to explain the acronym for a forward operating base to these elite soldiers, "we will establish at the same time the operation commences in a national forest north of the location. Depending on air assets available, as soon as the targets are recovered we will then exfil everyone back to the FOB and hold that until we can get a ride home."

He looked up, waiting for any questions or problems to be pointed out that he hadn't considered. Nobody offered any.

"Logistics and communications are our two biggest headaches. We are planning a mission relying on air assets we don't have yet, and once the mission starts the radio blackout will pose many unforeseen issues. On our own we can deal with it, but with the other forces we need to bring in to make this happen, if we don't get this right, then I'm rather afraid it has cluster fuck stamped all over it, sir."

Michaels nodded his head in agreement. "I agree. This mission is top of the priority list so I'm sure any request of ours will be met will full cooperation." He nodded toward the two majors. "If you two come with me we will get the Americans and Canadians up to speed on what we are up to. Captains, I don't need to tell you this but go and get your boys ready and all equipment squared away. Also, make a list of any equipment we do not have and need, and I will do my best to fulfil it."

He paused and laughed. "And please tell the men to keep their sticky bloody fingers in their pockets until at least after the mission. The Americans and Canadians really are on our side this time, and I want to keep it that way. If anyone is discovered to have 'just found' something that belongs to someone else, the punishment I will think up will be just as inventive and twice as painful as their story of how they came across it."

"You heard the general," Ginge said with a smirk, "I don't want to see anyone with an AT4 or something else they just happened to *find*."

CHAPTER
TWENTY

WEST COAST OF THE UNITED STATES

Ports, untouched by the bombing, but quickly taken control of by the Chinese, were rapidly filling with soldiers and equipment as the ships disgorged their cargoes as quickly as the facilities would allow, before moving aside to make way for the next waiting ship.

Tens of thousands of men climbed into vehicles as soon as they were unloaded, or marched away in formation to board the hundreds of yellow school buses, requisitioned by the Chinese to transport the newest wave of reinforcements to hundreds of locations across central and western United States. Requisitioned Air China passenger jets, which had been flying soldiers initially straight from China, began distributing more soldiers to locations further inland. Every ship that docked or airplane that landed added more numbers to the hundreds of thousands already stamping their boots over American soil.

"Yes, General Welch, we are in position," answered Commodore Phillipe James, commander of the Canadian Pacific fleet.

"Understood, Commodore. You are free to proceed as soon as you receive confirmation the other forces are in position."

"Affirmative, sir," James replied. "We will await the signal."

"Good hunting and God speed. Out," replied the general as he disconnected the call and turned to the officer at his side. "Update?"

"Sir, the Russians have one cruiser and three destroyers, and we currently have four Arleigh Burkes just outside the radar detection range of the Chinese blocking force. More are on the way. The littoral-class ships with their low radar profile have managed to sneak in closer without being detected. Our subs have also slipped in as close as they dare. As soon as they act on the Canadian feint we will be ready to strike."

They watched the large screens showing the positions of all the allied ships as they closed in on the coast. It was a waiting game. He trusted the commanders who were putting themselves into harm's way to know when the time to strike was.

"Sir? Admiral O'Reilly on the line," a communications officer said.

General Welch pressed a button on the control panel in front of him. "Go ahead, Jim, you are on speaker."

"Sir. We are in position. Permission to go?"

The general stared at the screen for a few moments. This operation they had called "Operation Chinese Laundry" was going to be the first major strike against the Chinese. Its name stuck after an aide suggested it tongue in cheek after General Welch summed the mission by saying it should hang them out to dry.

"Granted, Admiral. Go get the bastards."

"Thank you, General, we will."

CHINESE TYPE 002 CARRIER, OFF THE COAST OF CALIFORNIA

Captain Wayne Grant awoke to the sound of Klaxons blaring throughout the ship. Fully alert within seconds of waking, he threw on his clothes and ran toward the operations room. As he ran, the rumbling and whooshing of rockets being launched reverberated through the ship. He flattened himself against a bulkhead as a group of sailors ran past, donning flash hoods and helmets as they hurried to whatever post they had when action stations was called.

"Now it starts," he muttered acidly to himself. "I *knew* it wasn't over yet."

The operations room was hive of quiet, determined activity.

The Klaxon was still blaring, calling all hands to action stations, but inside the room it could barely be heard. They were the ones who activated the alarm, so it did not need to be drowning out the voices within, lest an urgent command or report be misheard or misunderstood. Sailors sat at their allocated stations monitoring the screens, some talking rapidly through their headsets, others watching monitors, pressing buttons, or adjusting dials.

The officer in charge stood at a desk in the center of the room. His job was to collate all the different and varied information and report to the captain who was most likely on the bridge, not in a windowless highly protected room, deep in the bowls. The captain could only see to the horizon whereas those in the operations room could see far beyond that, using radars and other highly sensitive and advanced equipment.

Wayne Grant knew that if he was to find out what was going on, the operations center was where he needed to be. Also, the coward in him knew it was the safest place to be. Its armored walls and advanced fire protection systems would enable it to remain operational even if the ship was heavily damaged. The officer in charge scowled at him as he entered and then turned away to keep on top of all the information that was being channeled to him.

Grant stood against a wall out of the way and listened to and watched what was going on, and rapidly understood they were under attack from ships to their north. Three Canadian frigates had entered their radar umbrella and at extreme range launched a volley of harpoon missiles at the Chinese fleet. When the ships were first detected, they were identified and plotted but no further action was taken. They were not at war with Canada and with instructions not to treat them as hostile they observed and no more.

Radio calls for them to turn around and steam away went unanswered. The captain had just ordered a flight of Shenyang J15 fighters to take off and investigate further when the missile launches were detected. The ship's automated point defense systems took over control and launched its own missiles, sending them flying towards the Canadians at supersonic speeds to destroy the incoming harpoons.

Grant knew the capabilities of the ship and the others forming the rings of protection around those currently unloading at the American ports. He could not understand what the Canadians thought they were doing. Three puny outdated frigates could not take on the power they were facing unless there were bigger hands to play. The point defense missiles fired were computer-controlled fire-and-forget munitions. The computers worked out the probability of a kill and if it fell below one hundred percent it automatically launched another.

The ship's system linked with all the other ships in the fleet and they worked together without the need for human input to destroy any incoming threat. At least three missiles fired from different trajectories were aimed at each incoming one.

A sailor at another station called out the hits as one by one the nine harpoon missiles launched from the Canadian ship were destroyed. The officer in charge barked an order. Grant, fluent in Mandarin, understood what was being said.

A sailor at one of the terminals replied, "Targets plotted. Frigates 530 and 619 also have good acquisition. Recommend multiple launch, sir. They are turning away and increasing speed." The officer talked rapidly through his headset. He was requesting permission to attack the Canadian frigates.

Another sailor shouted, "Sir. Four aircraft detected inbound seventy-five miles and closing fast. No transponder signals being received. Computer calculates them to be low-profile high-speed targets. High probability of being enemy fighter planes."

The officer relayed this information to the admiral of the fleet who was on the bridge six decks above him. He finished talking to his superior with, "Yes, sir," and then shouted to the room, "Launch at target ships. Plot air targets and engage if they come within twenty-five miles."

He then turned to the American standing in the corner and said, "You Westerners are foolish. Do you think that a few ships can do any harm to us? Every missile you fired at us has been blown out of the sky and now you send a few airplanes against us."

He paused and looked up at the low bulkhead as the distinctive sound of an airplane launching from the flight deck rumbled through the ship's hull. "Our fighters are launching to meet this pathetic threat head on. Soon they will see who the true global power is."

Grant was a fighter pilot at heart, and even though he had betrayed his country he still knew and respected the capabilities of his former countrymen. His role as advisor led him many times to tell his new masters to never underestimate what they were up against.

He looked at the officer with distain. "I am on your side if you haven't noticed. This attack is a feint."

The officer erupted at him, "A feint! What do you mean? They have launched nine missiles at us and not one came within thirty miles of our ships. The rest of your navy has run away and are in hiding with trembling knees waiting to surrender to us. Our ships are now chasing the Canadians away; our missiles will reduce them to burning hulks. It will show the rest of the world what will happen if anyone tries to stand in our way. America is *ours*." He clenched a fist as he finished his vitriol.

Grant, annoyed at the stupid arrogance of the man, bit back. "Do you really think it is going to be this easy? We do not do suicide missions. If the Canadians have attacked and are turning away, it is for a reason. Can't you see that? This is just the beginning, they are drawing you away, dividing us further. It is the oldest trick in the book and your arrogance is making you fall for it."

CHAPTER TWENTY-ONE

KENTUCKY

The Southern Kentucky militia had not fought the Chinese yet, but they had been far from idle. As soon as the reports of the bombs came in, and the destruction was seen on the television, the men and women of the militia had sprung into action; they had quietly gathered up supplies, loaded their trucks and cars, and had headed for the secluded campsites nestled in the Kentucky Hills.

Over a thousand men, women, and children were scattered in camps, hunting cabins, and compounds of all sizes throughout the vastness of the Black Mountain region. They came from all works of life across the socio-economic divide, but they all held the same belief: one day they would need to push back against government oppression and tyranny.

They did not consider themselves revolutionaries or traitors, quite the opposite. They felt they were the true American patriots, ready to defend their rights and homes to protect the America they thought it should be. Once they had paid their taxes and obeyed the reasonable laws of life, they should be left alone to pursue the American dream of democracy, rights, liberty, opportunity, and equality.

They'd always thought that one day it would be the corrupt government who sought to take away their God-given rights as American citizens, and they would be called to fight. The shock that it was foreign invaders who had nuked their cities and wanted to take everything away from them, took them some time to rationalize and alter their outlook on what they had joined the militia for.

Their numbers swelled as more joined. Ordinary citizens who would never have countenanced being part of any fringe militia decided to load their guns, pack everything they could into their vehicles, and take their families to seek out the militias that were rumored to be gathering in the mountains.

What to do next was the only thing they disagreed on. Some wanted to vent their anger immediately, searching out and killing the invaders who were taking control of innumerable cities, towns, and villages under the guise of their humanitarian effort.

Others, those with more strategic military knowledge, urged caution knowing organization was the key to success. The cooler heads prevailed, persuading everyone that first they needed to secure their position and then they could observe and plan the best way to fight back.

Lookout posts and bunkers that covered every approach to the wilderness they now called home were constructed. Roads were blocked, or charges were set on trees and hillsides so that a press of a button would make them impassable.

Many had served and understood that 'defense in depth,' meaning not just a single layer of lookout posts and bunkers, would be essential. Overlapping fields of fire were created and every road or trail had a system of fallback positions in case they were in danger of being overrun.

Training in basic tactics and fire discipline was given to the new arrivals if they had no military experience. The militia met regularly and trained for a whole host of scenarios, so they tried to impart as much of the wisdom and experience they had gathered over the years on the new arrivals as quickly as possible.

Working everyone hard each day, the work progressed rapidly, until they deemed that even with their limited numbers and the weapons they had (most legal, some not so that were brought out from storage now that fear of Federal interference had disappeared) they would be able to defend and repel an attack by a far stronger force.

Escape routes were mapped and planned, just in case, to take them deeper into the wilderness if any attack against them looked likely to succeed. When the work was deemed acceptable by the leadership they began to look outwards again.

Intermittent contact had been made with other militias around the country via ham radio. Comfort was taken from the fact that other groups were all doing much the same. Often distrustful of other groups, the transmission, asking for leaders of the various militias up and down the Appalachian range to meet for a war council, was initially met with suspicion.

As far as they knew it could be a trap set up by the invaders to cut the heads off the groups that their intelligence must know were gathering. Only after more conversations and information exchanges did they satisfy themselves that the request was valid.

Leland had arrived in Kentucky whilst all the preparation work was being undertaken. He was known to most of the leaders, some just by reputation, and had served with others, so his acceptance into the inner circle was quick and smooth.

He did not stop or deny the rumors that he had been involved in a far more secretive group of patriots, but instead used it to build his reputation. He and Cobb had quietly discussed what they would and would not say so no holes could be found in their cover story of why they had been in New York when the attacks began. They simply said they were in New York to meet up with arms dealers who had a pipeline to access weaponry currently unavailable to them.

News of the terrorist attacks in New York had never been linked to any American group and was all blamed as a Chinese diversion wholly created by them. It was the truth after all; they just failed to omit the part the Movement played in allowing it to happen.

Leland was asked if he wanted to be one of the small group of leaders to go to the Holly River Base. He refused, claiming his time would be better spent training the militia. Knowing there was going to be government leaders and current serving members of the military there, who may have more information on him than he knew, it was a risk he was not prepared to take. Accepting his reasoning he was given command of the militia whilst the others left in ATVs and pickups loaded with fuel and supplies, using the myriad of tracks and trails that wound through the mountains to reach Holly River.

Leland, along with most of the community, gathered to watch them leave. Everyone had a sense of anticipation. They felt strong and united, invincible in the stronghold they had created; ready to take the fight to the enemy. Leland knew the reality of what was to come would be far more brutal and terrifying than those that had not experienced combat realized. He was ready though. It was time to start doing what he enjoyed most.

Killing.

CHAPTER TWENTY-TWO

Troy cautiously approached Caldwell using the same route he had before. The road was clear, so they risked travelling closer. Hiding and camouflaging the trucks in a dense copse of woods not far from the road, he and his men set out on foot to cover the last few miles. Silently and stealthily, they worked their way into a position that gave a good view of the town. They worked in pairs, each one taking their turn to adopt a position of cover and raise their weapon as the other moved. They leapfrogged one another in a silent display of perfectly trained infantry troops which showed Gardner that he had less work than he anticipated to make the rag-tag unit a cohesive one.

At first glance everything looked normal. It was only when he studied the town through his binoculars that the true picture emerged. The only vehicles on the streets were military. Even though they were American vehicles the soldiers manning the machine guns on them certainly weren't; their uniforms showed they were Chinese. Trained to lie unmoving, they observed, making mental notes to write down later, building up a picture of what was going on.

The patrols were in strength; multiple vehicles drove in convoys around the area, all armored and all with a full complement of soldiers inside. Never deviating from a set route, they were only patrolling the immediate area around the base. It was a defensive posture, not going out looking for trouble, but maintaining a small perimeter to stop any threats getting close.

The base was bustling with activity. Forklift trucks and heavy machinery were raising and thickening the walls made of earth-filled gabions that surrounded the base. Large sandbagged emplacements were being built inside the compound by soldiers who were clearly working fast and with purpose. Motionless, Troy lay still for hours calculating the enemy forces and disposition until his sergeant, who was by his side, nudged him and directed his attention to the edge of the town.

He kept his binoculars pointing in the indicated direction until he saw two men appear from the side of a building, crouching low, from where his sergeant had spotted them hiding. They were cautiously making their way into town.

Troy knew with inevitability what was going to happen. The Chinese patrols stuck to a regular pattern and timing. He glanced at his watch knowing what the answer was going to be. The next patrol would appear behind them in the next two minutes. The wide-open street would give them very few options if caught in the open to escape. He could do nothing but watch. He was too far away to shout, and if he fired his weapon as a warning it would give their position away.

Willing them to hide, he was staring at them so hard, it was like he was trying to send them a telepathic message. But it was too late. With dreaded fasciation he watched as the first of the patrol vehicles rounded the corner behind them. Too late they noticed it and were caught in the open.

He watched the shock on their faces as they desperately looked around for a means of escape. Finding nowhere close, they turned and ran. He decreased the magnification on his binoculars, so he could see both the men and the Humvee with a soldier manning the fifty cal. The vehicle sped up, rapidly closing the gap between them. He was just beginning to think that they wanted to capture or question them when the soldier on the machine gun opened fire. The two fleeing men stood no chance against heavy bullets fired at such close range and their mutilated corpses fell to the road.

It took a few seconds for the heavy booming sound of the gun firing to reach them.

The sound of multiple guns firing made him snap back to look at the base. Every gun emplacement on the walls was pouring fire indiscriminately into the surrounding area until eventually it petered out and stopped.

They are on edge and expecting attack, thought Troy as he lay there. *The locals, if there are any alive, are on a strict curfew. Those two men were shot without any attempt to stop and question them. If the rest of the Chinese forces are acting this way, sheltering in their bases and not controlling the area, then we need to press the advantage and do our best to keep them bottled up where they can do no more harm.*

Troy had seen enough, it was time to investigate the camp they were meant to liberate. He gave a few hand signals and he and his sergeant slid back from their position and joined the men who were scattered in a defensive position around his location.

Toby sat on the dirt next to Harris, who had positioned himself on the bottom rung of the rough ladder they had used to scale the fence. He wanted to discourage any who wanted to break out before their scouts reported back. Toby had been telling Harris how he wanted to try and get back to his uncle in California as he was the only family he had.

"Toby, do you know how far California is? It's gotta be a thousand miles at least from here. Face it, dude, there is *no* way we are going to get there on our own."

Toby looked at Harris with a grin on his face. "Did you just say 'we'?"

Harris was a little shocked himself to realize he had. He had grown to like the young man who, at first, he had thought was weak and annoying. After caring for him after the beating he had taken when they were first captured he had continued to assume the role as his protector in the camp. Harris had never been close to anyone since leaving the army and taking the job as a security officer. Always the solitary individual, even as an only child to elderly parents who died in a car accident when he was in Afghanistan. The army had given him the only feeling of camaraderie he ever had.

Two tours in Afghanistan, though, were enough for him and he handed in his papers and retreated into the solitary life he led now. That was until Toby and Marissa entered his bunker and his life. He assumed the role of protector and if not a father figure, then a big brother.

He replied, "You don't expect me to trust you to get there all on your own, do you? I think you would find it hard to find your way out of an open door in a ten-foot by ten-foot room on a sunny day."

Toby was still smiling at him. "Ah, come on, big man. What you meant to say is that you'd miss my wit, charm, and natural good looks."

Harris looked at him. "And that, Toby, is why I thought you were an irritating little dumbass when I first met you. If I were you, I'd shut up before I change my mind."

He turned around and looked down the road in the direction the two scouts had gone. "Come on guys, where are you?" he complained softly to the air in general. "If we don't get out of here and get some food, and more importantly water, then most of us are going to be too weak to make it."

They both sunk into silence as they stared down the road. Toby eventually leaned up against the ladder next to Harris and slipped into a fitful sleep. Harris stayed alert, one eye on the road and one eye on Toby.

The not so distant burst of firing followed by the crescendo of many more guns joining in roused the whole camp from the stupor they had sunk in to and created mass panic. Harris, this time, could not stop the crowd as they surged the ladder. They pushed him aside, knocking him to the floor as they fought each other in their desperation to escape.

They both tried to plead with them, but reason had gone out of their panic-filled minds. Fearful of Toby getting crushed, Harris placed a protective arm around his shoulder for support and pushed his way out of the throng. Both stood watching as the camp emptied itself and scattered in all directions.

Toby stood swaying next to Harris in the empty yard watching the last man run wildly down the road. He would have stumbled and fallen if his large friend had not placed an arm around his shoulder. They said nothing for five minutes.

Toby looked around. "What do we do now?"

"We wait. That firing came from the direction of the town. Those idiots could have waited until we had a better idea of what direction to head in. If there is any more firing, it'll probably be aimed at them. We work out where it came from and go in the opposite direction."

They turned and sat in the shade of one of the roughly built structures in the camp. Toby drifted off again, the adrenaline rush of trying to stop the others escaping wearing off and leaving his body the exhausted, malnourished shell it had become.

Harris caught some movement out of the corner of his eye. Three figures in camouflage appeared from the undergrowth and, staying low with their weapons held ready, ran toward the gate.

Harris nudged Toby awake and helped him to his feet. "What's the matter? Toby muttered weakly.

Harris was smiling. He knew the soldiers approaching were elite troops just by the way they moved and how they dressed. When he was in Afghanistan he had come across special forces soldiers several times. They exuded that aura of calm and quiet competence that as a young man thrust into the terror and chaos of a war zone for the first time, he could only one day hope to achieve half as well.

"The cavalry has arrived, my friend, the cavalry has arrived."

They both slowly walked toward the gate. One of the soldiers pointed his weapon toward them. Harris raised his arm in the universal sign of welcome, and the soldier lowered his weapon a fraction but still kept it aimed at them. The other soldier was watching the back of the third who was fiddling with the padlock. Once he succeeded, he unwound the chain and lifted the locking bar from its brackets, throwing it aside. The three slid through the gap in the gate and with their weapons still searching for threats, approached the two lone inmates.

One of them spoke. "Where is everyone?"

Harris looked at him. He could tell he was the one in charge. "It's, err, it's just us," he admitted hesitantly. "They didn't wait for the scouts I had sent out to come back; they all panicked when the firing started half an hour ago and rushed the fence."

Troy looked at the roughly built ladder made of pieces of wood tied together with blankets. "You *built* that?"

"Yeah. When the Chinese pulled out yesterday we needed a way out of the camp, so I got everyone together and built it. I sent a few locals over the fence to scout the area to identify the best route for us to get out of here if we needed to. Then all that firing started and they all panicked. I tried to stop them but there was nothing I could do; they rushed the ladder and virtually climbed over each other to escape."

"Why didn't you two go too?" Gardner asked.

"Well," Harris said, suddenly worried that he had done the wrong thing, "I decided to see if any more firing started and then we'd head in the other direction."

Toby's legs could not support him anymore and he collapsed onto the ground beside Harris. More of Gardner's men had appeared from the bush and were, without any commands, setting up a perimeter around him.

Troy crouched down beside Toby. "Is he alright?"

"Not really, buddy. We have been together since all this shit began. He's still recovering from a beating he received when we got caught and he tried to protect a friend who was travelling with us," he explained. "I'm getting worried about him, he has been struggling to eat and is getting weaker and weaker. An English guy who was working in the camp gave him some peanut butter a few days ago and that made a difference for a short time."

Troy interrupted. "You met Cal?"

Harris looked confused. "Who?"

"The British dude? He was sent in by us to fetch some intel out of the camp. We were all set to liberate you and the other camps around here yesterday but got called off at the last minute. I requested we come back today to observe and gather more intel for when we get the go to liberate them."

He looked around and shrugged. "Guess we're too late now."

The sound of firing coming from the direction of town stopped any further conversation. It built up and the booms of explosions shook the air. Troy waved toward the sounds.

"The Chinese are hunkered down in their base and working hard to improve the defenses," he explained. "The firing you heard was them killing two men we observed entering the town. They are so nervous the whole camp began firing in all directions as soon as the first shots were fired. I'm sorry to say they were probably the scouts you sent out, and if others from the camp went that way then I imagine it's them who they are firing at now. It does answer your question though as to which way to go. Anywhere but toward town is my recommendation."

"Okay," Harris said with a knitted brow. "Err, mind if I ask who the hell you guys are?"

"Sorry," Gardner said as he extended a gloved hand, "Troy Gardner, Captain US Combined Applications Group." He saw the confused look on Harris' face deepen. "Special Forces," he added, seeing the dawn of realization wash over him.

The firing continued for a time then slowly diminished. Troy knew the unarmed civilians would have stood no chance and been slaughtered in the face of the firepower the Chinese had. Outwardly calm, internally he was seething with rage. The mission to liberate the camps had been cancelled and now the blood of innocent civilians was on his hands. He stood silently staring in the direction of the town and the massacre he knew would have taken place there.

Could he and his men do something to extract revenge? He was pulled back from his thoughts by Harris. "What were you going to do with us when you got us out of the camps?" he asked out of genuine curiosity.

"The plan was to help you get north of here. There are plenty of towns that are free of the Chinese. Messengers have been sent to request these people take in refugees. Once there, we are going to start building the resistance movement. Plenty of folks will have military experience, we just need to get them organized and formed into effective groups. If we are going to kick the fucking Chinese out of our country, then we will need everyone who can hold a gun on our side."

"Count me in, sir. I guess there ain't going to be much need for security guards for a while, so I may as well reenlist."

"Where did you serve?"

Harris pulled himself straighter. "Marines, sir. I was with One-Eight. Two tours of Afghanistan. Started off in Sangin and it got a whole lot shittier from there. Got out after my second tour and have been doing security ever since."

"Well we could sure use you. We put the call out and our base in West Virginia is getting new arrivals every day. There are plenty out there looking for some payback."

Toby was being tended to by a soldier. He had come around and was sipping from a canteen and eating a high-energy bar the soldier had given him. The water and food was already helping him; he looked slightly better and was able to sit up unaided.

"What about Marissa? She must be in a camp near here. We must try to get to her if we can," Toby said.

Troy looked at Harris. "Marissa?"

"She was with us from the beginning; it's why Toby got a

beating when we got captured. He took offence at how the Chinese were handling her." Harris then told Troy a brief version of their story from him allowing them into his bunker and their escape from Cleveland to their capture.

Toby staggered up to Troy. "Come on Harris, let's go and get Marissa. Her camp cannot be far away."

He walked unsteadily through the soldiers and headed toward the open gate. Harris turned to Troy, shrugged, and started to follow him. Harris caught up to Toby in a few steps. They had reached the gate when a shout from Troy stopped them.

He walked up to them. "Look," he said bluntly, "like it or not I feel like you're my responsibility now. Hold on for a while and we will accompany you to find the women's camp. Do you know where it is?"

Toby looked at Harris and shook his head. "Not really. There were rumors from others in the camp that the women are being held in another prison close by."

Troy knew from studying the maps and intel that the town's second prison was further out of town not far from where they were currently. He reached into a pocket and pulled out a map and studied it, refreshing himself on the layout of the area.

He called his sergeants around him and they spent a few minutes discussing strategies. Harris and Toby stood watching. Toby was feeling stronger with every minute that passed, the energy bars he had eaten having an immediate effect and the liters of water he had drunk had rehydrated his parched body.

Troy approached them. "I'm sending a few guys back to the overwatch position we had on the town to report on any Chinese movements. Once they give the all clear we will approach the prison." He looked at Toby. "You feel strong enough to come?"

Toby nodded. "I was heading there when you stopped us, wasn't I? A marathon may be out of the question for a while but yes, if we are looking for Marissa then I'll make it."

"Captain, do not worry about him, I'll carry him if I have to. Let's just get on with it."

Troy looked at them both and smiled. "I'm sure you will, buddy," he said with a smile, "I'm sure you will."

Chapter Twenty-Three

Swall, CA

Sergeant Eddie Edmunds drove fast. His passenger held on as he negotiated the tight turns leading away from the main highway that ran the length of the San Joaquin Valley on the road to the town of Swall. Satisfied that the defenses he and the town had been busy building to protect themselves from any further Chinese encroachments were as good as the limited time and materials available allowed, he had decided to investigate the local area.

The geography of the area helped. The single road that led to the pretty town cut through a steep-sided wooded valley. Using construction equipment and local farmers' tractors and excavators they had blocked the road and created a system of earthen berms, foxholes, and bunkers. With the addition of the heavy machine guns and other arms gathered from the Chinese soldiers they had poisoned, they should, if not attacked by heavy armor, effectively protect the town.

His worry was the people he had available to man these and the other defenses they had built. Most people with military experience had been rounded up and imprisoned in the first stages of the invasion. Along with the sick and elderly, they had been murdered in their tens of thousands by the Chinese in their inhuman policy of ridding themselves of any who may pose a threat to their plans.

Subsequently he was left with civilians who had little experience of firearms manning bunkers and guard posts armed with modern military weapons. Showing them how to operate these weapons had been the easy task, but how they would act when under fire was unknown.

Soldiers train for years under simulated battle conditions, so fire discipline, how to deal with a jammed or inoperable weapon, and any of the other myriad fast-changing situations that happen under the stress of battlefield conditions were a taught skill.

He'd only had days to impart his years of knowledge and skill on the willing but untried locals and was under no illusion that as soon as the bullets started coming downrange, their defenses, no matter how well built and strong, could easily be overrun.

He just hoped that the knowledge they were defending their homes, family, and country would give them the courage and steel to remain fighting when everyone's natural instinct would be to run and hide.

Eddie, along with and old farmer called Wayne, who had fought in the Vietnam war, left the valley and ventured further afield. Wearing civilian clothes and with their guns well hidden, armed with a travel permit stamped and signed by one of the townspeople who had been entrusted to work in the local commander's office, they drove a pickup truck loaded with local produce. They hoped that if stopped the cover story that they were transporting foodstuffs to another location would be deemed genuine enough to allow them to pass scrutiny.

Happily surprised that they had had no contact from any other Chinese forces investigating why their little area of control had gone quiet, they needed more intelligence about what was going on in the wider world. The only assumption he could make was that the administration of linking and coordinating the huge array of men and materiel they already had in country had not yet caught up with the speed they had assumed control.

Choosing not to take the main highway, they had driven north using roads that ran parallel. The first checkpoint they came across was fifteen miles from their town in a small village. The bored sentries accepted their cover story and barely glanced at the pass Eddie handed over, waving them through with barely a pause.

Wayne told him to stop at the small store in the village that sold trinkets to tourists and basic supplies to locals to save them the longer journey to the larger shops in the next town. He knew Bobby the owner and wanted to check in on him, telling Eddie he had known him for years and he could be trusted. Eddie parked the truck outside and, trying to look as casual as they could, they walked into the store.

The proprietor, leaning on the long counter that ran along one side of the store, looked up as they entered, the small bell on the door unnecessarily announcing their arrival.

He smiled as he recognized his old friend. "Wayne, my friend," he called out. "What brings you to these parts? I haven't seen many from Swall since our unwelcome guests arrived."

Wayne and Eddie nervously glanced around, a few people were in the store picking goods off the shelves. Noticing their reaction, he waved his arm toward them. "Don't worry, you are among friends here."

Eddie, conscious of maintaining their cover story, spoke loudly enough for the others to hear as he shook his hand. "We have been ordered to deliver produce to stores in the area. Do you have need for anything?"

Bobby noticed the look on Wayne's face and lifted the hatch on the counter, keeping up the conversation. "We could always use more, why don't you come through to my office so we can discuss this further."

As they followed him through the door he called to his young assistant who was sweeping the floor to mind the counter whilst he conducted some business. Ten minutes later Wayne and Eddie had fully updated him on the events in Swall. His elation that something was being done gave Eddie the reassurance that the man could be trusted. Bobby then told them all he knew about their situation. The Chinese only had a small detachment in the village who reported to the larger garrison in the next town, ten miles further up the road.

Since the rounding-up of locals in the first few days of the invasion the villagers had quietly gone about their business trying not to get in the way. The villagers had met and discussed what they could do, but most of the fighting-age men had been detained and hadn't been seen since they had been herded into trucks and driven away, so their capability to do anything had been reduced. They chose to carry on with their daily lives but be uncooperative and subtly hinder the Chinese in any way they could. Bobby expressed shame at how little they had done compared to the citizens of Swall.

Twenty minutes later they were back in the truck, a few boxes of vegetables lighter, but with an agreement that Bobby would start to rally the locals to prepare in any way they could to begin to fight back when the time was right.

Avoiding the main road, they visited a few more villages that lay between Swall and the highway, and if their instincts told them they could trust the locals they told the news of their rebellion in the hope that it would spread. Eventually with the back of the truck empty they decided they had learned enough, and it was time to head back.

The numerous cups of coffee they had accepted caused them to both need to answer the call of nature and so they pulled over to the side of the road. Standing, directing his stream, Eddie looked across from their elevated position down over the flat valley to the distant highway.

The distance was too great to see any detail, but he could make out a lot of movement on the road. He turned and picked up the binoculars from the dash of the truck. To his dismay he could see the highway stretching into the distance was full of military trucks and yellow school buses all heading up the valley. At every junction some vehicles peeled off from the convoy and headed along roads that led toward other towns and villages along the valley.

Still looking at the magnified view he called to Wayne, "It looks as if they are reinforcing the garrisons along the whole valley. If each of those buses and trucks are carrying soldiers there must be thousands of them."

In silence they watched the progress of the convoy that distance made look agonizingly slow.

"Shit! Fifteen, no twenty vehicles have turned off at the Swall junction. We need to get back *now*! They can only be heading our way."

They both turned and ran back to the truck. Its tires screeched and with its engine revving Eddie put his foot to the floor and the pickup truck shot up the road toward their hometown.

Racing along the road Eddie thought about their situation. He had seen no armor in the convoy for which he was thankful. They had a large quantity of shoulder-launched anti-tank rocket launchers which were similar to the ones he had been trained on. Needing to be operated by troops in a battlefield situation their operation was not hard to understand and with his knowledge of Chinese he understood the operating instructions stamped on them.

The option not to fight did not exist. If the invaders discovered what they had done their lives would be forfeit anyway. Their only course of action was to defeat them or die trying. Their truck screeched to stop by the barricade and Eddie was pleased to see the locals manning it were alert due to the many guns pointing toward him. He was even more pleased no one pulled their trigger.

Not wanting to waste the time opening the barrier to let the vehicle through, he and Wayne, after grabbing the weapons they had hidden in the car, scrambled up the ladder he had shouted to be lowered. All eyes were on him as he stood in the center of the defenses they had constructed.

He raised his voice so all could hear him. "Twenty or so trucks and buses are heading this way. I can only guess it's reinforcements or replacements for the garrison here. We cannot let them through."

He let the statement to sink in for a moment; soon they

would be fighting the enemy.

"It's going to get real in a few minutes. We have the advantage of surprise and we must make the most of it. *Do not hold back*. We must keep the pressure on them and not allow them to get organized. If they do, then their training will take over and it will be all over for us.

"We are fighting to protect our families and friends. Once you open fire do not stop until there is no one left to shoot at. Those with rocket launchers, you know how to use them, take your time and aim straight. The signal to fire will be when I open fire. Everyone check your ammo and call out targets. Hold your fire and wait for my signal."

He turned to the group of men and women who were the designated reserve force, ready to replace their fallen friends or go where ever the battle dictated. "You guys hold here. When we need you though, do not hesitate—go to where you are told and fight hard no matter what you see."

He could not add any more. The training he had given was not sufficient and would not prepare them for the coming battle. He had to trust that their courage would last and give them the strength to fight. Faces grim with determination, the townsfolk looked at each other. Handshakes were exchanged, some hugged as longer friendships were acknowledged but they all hefted their weapons and, carrying extra ammunition or rocket launchers, headed to their allocated positions on the defenses, or waited to be called.

The few people who had military experience, whose age or good fortune had spared them from the Chinese purge, had become the captains in Sergeant Eddie Edmunds' militia. They spent their time walking between the firing positions, passing on a few last words of wisdom or encouragement before settling in to their own spot. Silence descended.

Eventually the revving of engines could be heard as the approaching vehicles negotiated the final few bends leading to their town. Eddie had laid out the road block with careful consideration. Bunkers and trenches lined the road leading up to the barricade, so fire could be brought to bear, not just on the lead element of anything that approached, but the flanks as well. Fields of fire had been cleared along the sides of the road to reduce available cover for an attacking force to shelter behind.

Standing in a firing position in the center of the line Eddie had to cast all doubts aside. He had done his best; he had to trust that everyone would do their duty to the best of their abilities.

Crouching down he watched as a lorry appeared around the corner and slowed as its driver realized the way ahead was blocked. He waited, the tube of the launcher in his hand, primed and ready to fire—it would only be a matter of a few seconds for him to raise it to his shoulder and fire. He could see the driver on his radio, seeking instructions from a superior. The roadblock had caught him by surprise and he was clearly unsure what to do next.

The driver put the bus into gear and moved forward again, getting closer with every second that passed. Eddie still waited; he needed to get as many of the vehicles into the kill zone as possible. Every meter mattered. Luckily for them the time of day worked in their favor. The sun was behind them, low in the sky, shining straight through the front windscreen of the truck making it harder for the driver to see clearly ahead. As it got closer the driver honked the horn as if to indicate he wanted the gate to open. Judging they had pushed their luck as far as they could, he knew the time to spring the trap was now.

Quickly checking the rocket launcher was still 'live' he stood up and took aim. It only took him a second to aim at the cab and fire. The rocket leapt from the launch tube and sped faster than the eye could follow to pierce the window of the truck and explode in a deadly fireball. Picking up another launcher, he aimed this time at the rear of the truck. In a matter of seconds it was a burning mangled wreck. Bodies, blown from the rear by the force of the explosion, lay unmoving on the road.

Seconds later more rockets flew toward other vehicles further along the convoy as people recovered from the shock of the first explosion and fired. Gunfire began to tear into the trucks and buses as everyone else opened up, belt-fed machine guns and assault rifles firing on fully automatic, smashing windows and puncturing the thin sides of the trucks and buses. The inexperience of the defenders showed as a lot of the rockets missed and exploded harmlessly away from the targets. Eddie just hoped that they had not inadvertently hit other defenders, but he knew that the explosions would still be adding to the mayhem and confusion their surprise attack had created.

Soldiers spilled from the trucks and return fire began zipping overhead or hitting their positions. The air became filled with falling leaves and splinters of bark as bullets shredded the trees around them. The battle now hung in the balance as the untrained, untested defenders fired wildly at the hundreds of trained battle-hardened veterans who, now recovering from the shock of being attacked unexpectedly, began to get organized and fight back. Outgoing fire began to dwindle as the defenders found themselves pinned down by returning fire.

Eddie was lobbing grenades at a group of Chinese soldiers who had reached the ditch at the side of the road and were laying down sustained and accurate fire at the positions around him. Bravely exposing himself to the incoming bullets, he threw his fourth grenade. He knew the advantage was being lost and something needed to be done. The incoming fire as they exploded in quick succession reduced, giving him the opportunity to fire a long burst, emptying his magazine at the Chinese who had thrown themselves flat to the ground. Others emerged from cover as the incoming fire reduced. They lined the foxholes, and fire from his sector began to rip into the attackers once more.

He screamed at those around him to keep firing as he leapt from his position and moved to the flanks to bolster the defenders who were still being pinned down by the increasing level of fire. With bullets hitting all around him as his movement attracted unwanted attention he dove into a foxhole where two terrified townsfolk were cowering, bullets hitting all around their position. Another lay dead in the bottom of the trench. The two alive were covered in the blood that had sprayed from the wound that had killed their friend.

An unused rocket launcher leaned against the side of the trench. Risking a glance over the lip of the trench, he identified where the fire was primarily coming from and spotted a group of about ten soldiers with guns blazing sheltering under a truck untouched by the rockets.

"Stand up and fight!" Eddie shouted at them, berating them for their cowardice. He picked up the rocket launcher, taking a few seconds to arm it ignoring the fire that was hitting all around them, then stood up and fired at the truck. The rocket exploded, shredding the men under it and the volume of fire coming toward them reduced significantly.

Grabbing the two cowering men he pulled them up and pushed their weapons back into their hands, screaming at them in his best sergeant's voice to get back into the fight. It worked. Eddie watched as their courage returned and they both, shouting incoherently, began to fire down on the Chinese again.

He slapped them on the back and leapt out of their trench to go to the next one along. Once again bullets kicked up the dirt and splintered the trees around him as he ran. Every time the defenders responded to his actions and encouragement. Instead of cowering, they stood up and faced their enemy. Slowly the fight began to swing back in their favor as more and more guns fired at the ever-reducing quantity of enemy soldiers.

Returning towards his original position he stopped at a fallen tree and from a new angle surveyed the battlefield. The increasing fire from the townsfolk had subdued the Chinese and those he could see were now mainly trying to hide from the bullets being fired from all directions. If one returned fire it immediately brought a lead-filled response from the townsfolk searching for a target.

He watched with dismay as a group of about twenty soldiers broke from the cover of a burning truck and made for the trees on the opposite side of the road to him. It was a coordinated move timed when sudden bursts of accurate counterfire from the Chinese made the defenders duck back into their holes. Four or five were hit before they reached the cover of the trees, but at least fifteen made it.

Knowing that the defenders would not stand a chance against the highly trained troops, he needed to act quickly. He ran down the line of defenses and shouted at every third person to follow him. It was leaving them thin on the ground but the counterattack, if allowed to get established, would finish them, so the risk was worth it.

Stopping behind the barricade he addressed the reserve force and those he had ordered to follow him. "They are outflanking the left-hand positions. At least fifteen made it to the tree line. We will advance along the left flank until we meet them. Stay in your squads as you have been shown and don't bunch up."

He could not explain fire and maneuver tactics to them, the only advantage they had was numerical and weight of firepower they could bring to bear. "If you see something just keep firing at it till it falls over or you see another target."

With no time to waste he waved them forward and led the group of mainly untried civilians toward the enemy. The sound of fighting to their right was now limited to brief exchanges. As they approached the first position he again told every third person manning it to grab their spare ammunition and join them, and those remaining to keep the Chinese in the convoy pinned down and to watch their left side, but not fire unless they were certain it wasn't them.

Indicating for everyone to spread out they advanced, gathering more from every foxhole until a series of explosions and screams of pain ahead in the woods made them stop. Hand signals would not work so all he could do was shout his instructions and hope that his voice was mistaken by the Chinese as coming from the defenders calling to each other.

Finding cover behind trees both standing and fallen, the forty townsfolk got ready to hold the line. It was only when gunfire ripped into their single line of defenders, hitting four of them, that they saw the Chinese advancing in small squads, overlapping each in the classic fire and maneuver discipline.

"Fire! Hold the line. Do not let them get through us," Eddie bellowed with more than a hint of desperation and panic in his voice.

For every Chinese soldier he saw getting hit at least three or four locals went down screaming in pain, clutching hands to wounds or more ominously lying still and silent.

He knew they were in a desperate position but was unable to do anything more than keep fighting until either they or their enemies were all killed. A blow to his left arm knocked him over. Looking at it as he lay on the ground he knew he had been hit by a bullet but felt no pain. Regaining cover behind a now bullet-splintered tree he held his rifle in one hand and emptied the magazine toward the enemy. His left arm was useless making it impossible for him to insert a new magazine once he had ejected the spent one, so he let it fall to the floor. He pulled his sidearm from its holster strapped to his leg and held it out in front of him.

He knew it was all over and they had been defeated. Understanding they were dead anyway as soon as the Chinese found out what they had done to their fellow countrymen, he decided he may as well take as many with him as he could before the end. Every single one he killed would be one less for another American to kill before they could take the country back.

The sounds of firing and voices cursing and screaming at the advancing Chinese told him a few others were still in the fight.

A soldier emerged from cover behind a tree, and Eddie raised his pistol and took aim but before he could pull the trigger a red mist of blood and brains blew from the side of his head and he crumpled to the floor. Another came into view, not pointing his weapon in his direction, but away to the left, further up the hill in a direction he knew no one should be. Again he fell to a well-aimed shot to the head. More distinctive booms of heavy caliber hunting rifles rang out.

Hope began to rise in Eddie. Someone was on the enemy's flank, firing into their exposed sides as they advanced toward them through the trees. Another broke cover knowing he was out-flanked by an unseen marksman; he tried to run back down the slope to the convoy but was brought down by Eddie emptying his pistol at him as he ran past.

As he fumbled trying to reload his gun one handed a voice called from further up the slope. "Don't shoot, we are approaching from your left. We think we got 'em all but there could still be one or two we haven't noticed."

No more fire was incoming and Eddie, who had eventually managed to reload his handgun, called back. "Okay. But watch your front for incoming rounds, there are still Chinese down on the road."

Holding his gun in one hand Eddie kept it pointing forwards.

Pain from the gunshot wound in his arm, that until now he hadn't felt, hit him like a hammer blow and he staggered. His left sleeve was soaked in blood, but he couldn't look at it yet, there was still more fighting to do.

Captain Li Wie looked around himself in despair. He could hear no more firing coming from the direction of the counterattack he had ordered in a last-ditch attempt to subdue the ambush they had driven into. Most of the men under his command lay dead or injured around him and he had no idea if any other officers had survived. Incoming fire still rang off the metal sides or hit the ground around the smoking truck he was under.

The two soldiers still with him were out of ammunition and he only had a few rounds left. He shouted out, calling for any soldier to respond, trying to figure out how many were still capable of fighting. He could hear his command being repeated by a few soldiers further down the convoy. He had no radio to issue or receive orders.

The last orders he had received were when they boarded the huge convoy of vehicles that drove away from the port where they had arrived. They were being driven to a town already under Chinese control where they would strengthen the garrison and await further orders.

The mood on the bus until the explosions and bullets started flying had been of excitement. They had been told that the

American invasion had been an unqualified success, the whole country was under their control and the mission was more a policing role, so they could begin to reap the rewards of their victory. He and the men in the bus gawked out of the window at the passing landscape, calling out landmarks or city and town names they had only seen or heard of in movies.

Now he found himself lying under a smoldering wreck of a bus, surrounded by dead and dying men, the shame and anger building up inside him in equal measure. He had been misled by their leaders; if they had known the Americans were fighting back they would have been more prepared and wouldn't have driven blindly into an ambush. He felt shame knowing most in his command had been killed and he had not been able to lead or protect them—he had failed them all.

Deciding to do the one action he could to protect his men he reached into a pocket and pulled out a light-colored silk scarf his mother had given him before he left his native land.

Waving it in front of him he crawled out from under the bus and stood up. Half expecting to be struck down by a volley of fire he shouted out one of the few English words he knew. "FRIEND, FRIEND!"

No bullets struck him. As he stood there waving his scarf, more soldiers up and down the ruined line of vehicles dropped their weapons and emerged to stand with their hands above their heads.

Tears of shame ran down his cheeks made worse by the cheering he could now hear coming from the trees around him.

Bobby, the man Eddie had met in his shop only a few hours before, helped him down the slope.

Wayne ran forward to help him when he saw who he was assisting. Eddie looked at Wayne and said weakly, the pain and blood loss from his injury making his words slur, "Bobby here just saved our asses. If he and the others from his village hadn't arrived when they did, we would have lost."

Still holding his pistol in one hand Eddie looked along the road at the locals who were guarding the surrendered soldiers. They had won but at a heavy cost, he knew many had given their lives to protect their town.

His vision faded, and he collapsed.

CHAPTER
TWENTY-FOUR

PACIFIC OCEAN

Sea Sparrow missiles launched from all the Canadian frigates as they ploughed through the seas at maximum revolutions heading away from the Chinese fleet. The fully automatic point defense systems took over, launching missiles and decoys to destroy or confuse the incoming Chinese anti-ship missiles heading toward them.

Commodore Phillipe James watched the information being relayed from the ship's operation room to a screen on the bridge. There was little he could do but trust the automated defense systems to counter the threat. They had launched their own missiles at extreme range on purpose, with no real hope of success, the only aim to create a diversion for the next stage in the plan.

He silently prayed that the incoming missiles which, from what he understood of their capabilities were also at the limit of their range, would not get through their own defenses. Calculating that it was now time to begin the next stage of the plan he picked up the handset next to his chair. Speaking directly to the commander of the squadron of CF-18 Hornets he told him to begin their mission.

The four CF-18s that had already entered the fray were dueling with the Chinese Shenyang J-15s launched from the carrier; missiles flew, and cannon fire ripped across the sky as they played their deadly game of cat and mouse, but that was a distraction intended to draw the Chinese away from the next threat. At the commander's order twenty CF-18s—that had been loitering behind the Canadian frigates out of radar contact of the Chinese— lit their afterburners and streaked into the battle. Carrying a mixed load of air-to-air and air-to-surface missiles, they gained altitude and sought their targets like an aerial pack of hunters.

The first missiles were launched at the anti-ship missiles speeding toward the Canadian vessels. They knocked more out of the sky, but still some got through and streaked toward the ships that were emptying their launchers at the honing-in ship killers. Onboard the ships the Phalanx close-quarter defense guns began spitting a solid stream of 20 mm cannon fire at the incoming missiles.

The ship's speakers broadcast the reports from the operations center. Initially, each reported hit had been met with cheers, but now an air of tense silence settled over the ship. With inevitability the commodore recognized they were not going to get them all and ordered the collision alert to sound. Knowing what they were attempting to do he had ordered every fifty-cal machine gun to be mounted on the decks.

"Port side open fire," he commanded through the ship's PA system, and immediately the distinctive deep chatter of multiple guns firing filled the air as thousands of bullets flew outwards in the hope that just one hit would destroy the incoming missile. The seas around all the ships filled with bullets hitting the wavetops sending up plumes of spray. An explosion on the horizon indicated at least one hit.

"Sir, the Vancouver has been hit!" a seaman shouted pointing off the starboard side of the ship.

The commodore rushed to the bridge window and, grabbing some binoculars, searched for the frigate that was under his command.

The fireball was still rising from the missile that had exploded in the bow of the Vancouver. It looked badly damaged, but ships were hard to sink in reality, and as long as the hull was not breached too badly, and if the fire could be brought under control, he knew there was chance to save it. There was nothing he could currently do but tell the radio operator to send a message that they would render aid when they could. They still had a battle to fight and the crew of the stricken frigate would have to rely on their own resources to control the damage.

He breathed a sigh of relief when the PA system announced, "No more missiles inbound."

He performed a quick evaluation of the progress so far in his head. His ships had done their duty and feigned an attack on the Chinese from the north, causing some to leave their positions and pursue them as they turned tail and steamed away at high speed after launching their missiles.

Even though one ship had been hit and was out of the fight, all the onboard defense systems had coped with the incoming missiles. The chance that, if faced with multiple targets, one or two might get through was a risk they had had to accept.

An old general would have probably said, "You can't make an omelet without breaking eggs." And that was true, but he would still have to live with the fact that the eggs were men and women under his command and most likely many had been killed when the Vancouver was hit.

It was time for phase three to begin. "Send the order to launch all remaining harpoons at the pursuing ships please."

His own ship juddered as more missile leapt from their tubes and, with engines sprouting long jets of flame, shot across the ocean to an enemy he had yet to see. Smoke trails led away from the other frigates and he experienced an emotional moment of pride as two missiles launched from the stricken Vancouver. It was still in the game despite the catastrophic damage it had received.

The Hornets turned the air battle quickly into a one-sided

slaughter as multiple air-to-air missiles turned the four J-15s to burning fireballs falling from the sky.

The four original CF-18s, low on fuel and ordnance, peeled off and went to find the waiting refueling plane before returning to their base in Canada. The rest continued pressing the attack, launching Maverick missiles at the multiple targets that showed on their targeting displays.

CHINESE TYPE 002 CARRIER, FIFTEEN MILES OFF THE COAST OF CALIFORNIA

The operations room of the carrier was in chaos. One moment they were tracking their outgoing missiles, the operator calling the countdown to impact, and the next multiple aircraft appeared, flying toward them at supersonic speeds.

One by one the four fighters they had launched blinked and disappeared from the screens and then over thirty more inbound missiles were detected.

The aircraft carrier was in the center of a multi-layered ring of defense provided by over sixty destroyers, frigates, and corvettes covering hundreds of square miles of ocean. Huge landing ships and converted cruise liners were disgorging their complements of men, armored vehicles, attack helicopters, and huge quantities of other stores at ports along the coast. Once they had they cleared the port, they joined the fleet of vessels and even though not heavily armed they carried defense weapons of all capabilities.

Twenty aircraft did not possess the strength to break through to them, but they could seriously damage or destroy many ships if not repulsed. The admiral in command of the Chinese fleet was on the bridge of the aircraft carrier following the flow of information that was relayed to him via screens or verbally from the ship's operation center.

"I don't care if the fighter pilots want to engage the Americans," he shouted angrily down the handset. "We need them to protect the carrier. Order them to remain on station. We have enough missiles to blow one hundred times more than they are sending at us out of the sky. I am not wasting precious planes because they want to show the American cowboys who has a bigger dick."

The duel between the incoming missiles and the fleet's defense systems was focusing the attention of the fleet's surveillance systems. Most of their sensor and radar capabilities was directed toward the Canadian attack. Other systems still maintained a 360-degree coverage, but there was so much incoming information they were struggling to compute all the data.

As the battle raged to the north, west, and south, the combined American and Russian surface fleet waited for the order to commence their attack. Deep beneath the waves each of the detected

Chinese submarines had a silent killer tracking its course with yet more submerged executioners stealthily creeping toward the outer ring of the Chinese ships.

CHEYENNE MOUNTAIN

General Welch and his Russian counterpart sat side by side in the cavernous control room at Cheyenne Mountain watching the information being relayed on the large screen in front of them.

The general sipped from the mug of coffee an aide continually kept full of the strong caffeine-filled black liquid and said quietly to Russian by his side, "I think we are about ready to commit. Do you agree, my friend?"

The Russian nodded. "Da, I agree Comrade General."

He called out, "Get me Admiral O'Reilly on the horn."

The voice of the admiral came through the speakers a few seconds later. "Doug. We're all set. Every sub is reporting targets acquired and locked. Those boys are catching up fast, but their tin cans aren't as good or as quiet as they think they are," he said with cruel glee. "All surface assets are in position. I'm just waiting for my gut to tell me it's time to press the button and then we will give those Communist bastards an ass kicking."

"Okay, Jim. Go get 'em." The general ended the call. Not one to waste words he knew the admiral had far more important tasks to do than waste time talking to him.

USS Ronald Reagan

Admiral O'Reilly sat back in his chair and mentally went through all aspects of the assault he had planned, checking for the one hundredth time that nothing had been missed. Understanding that no battle ever sticks to the plan after the opening salvo is fired, he knew that the time for planning was over and it was now time to commit tens of thousands of men and women and billions of dollars of the most advance military equipment built to battle.

He picked up the handset by the side of him and ordered the attack to begin.

Chinese Type 002 Carrier Operations Center

"Sir, multiple inbound surface contacts," a sailor shouted.

The officer in charge scowled at him. "I know, you fool," he snarled. "Do you think I don't know?"

The missiles fired from the Canadian ships and airplanes were wreaking havoc amongst the northern sector of their defenses. As intended, their point defense systems could not cope with the volume of incoming targets. Two destroyers and three frigates had been hit and were calling for urgent assistance, and many other ships had expended most of their munitions when their automated systems kept firing until the last incoming missiles were destroyed.

The officer was overwhelmed with too much information and multiple requests for orders and assistance that he had not comprehended what the young sailor was telling him. All ships, no matter how technologically advanced, were based around a modern idea of war where they may be attacking or defending themselves but only from or at a limited number of targets. The concept of a mass sea battle where the fleets of nations slugged it out across the oceans was thought to be a thing of the past, last fought in the Pacific campaign of World War II and considered impossible after the end of the Cold War.

Those battles of World War II were fought by airplanes and shell fire, both of which could be replenished at sea after the battle. Firepower on modern ships came from their missiles not their deck guns, which were mainly now limited to one, albeit powerful and with advanced targeting capabilities. The logistics of reloading the launch systems was a dangerous and complicated process that mostly needed to be done in a dockyard.

Many ships on the outer ring of the northern sector of the Chinese fleet, although they had effectively, except for the acceptable loss of a few ships, defeated the Canadian attack, were now low on missiles and vulnerable to another.

"Sir, missiles inbound from other vectors," the sailor tried again.

This made the officer stop and run to his screen.

Another sailor shouted out, "Detecting torpedoes in the water. Not ours, sir. Calculating targets now."

He waited for the information to display on his screen. "None heading for the fleet, displaying tracks now." He paused and held his hands to his headphones as if to help him hear more clearly. "Detecting one, no *two* explosions, unknown source."

The officer shouted in anger, "They are targeting our submarines you idiot!"

SONG-CLASS SUBMARINE

The fate of the captain, his submarine, and the men who served under him was similar to many of the other submarines the Chinese had deployed to protect the invasion fleet.

Submerged, they had formed a hidden outer ring around the fleet, shadowing its progress across the vast emptiness of the Pacific Ocean, all the time searching for any contact, however distant, that may indicate an enemy submarine probing the net they had thrown around the surface ships. Detecting occasional contacts which had vanished when investigated further, he was confident the seas around them were clear of any underwater threats.

The last news he had received was that the American

president had been captured and was about to sign the surrender. He would not have become a captain on one of his homeland's most advanced submarines if he had not been a loyal party member, and so believed, without question, the propaganda and rhetoric spewed forth by his commanders as to the success of the operation and how the United States was a beaten and cowed animal just waiting for them to control.

The captain stood in the control room as it glided quietly through the deep and was proud of the part he and his crew had played in his country's latest adventure. His mind wandered briefly as he imagined the stories he would tell his grandson as he sat on his knee, listening to him recount the time he was a submarine captain and invaded America, when the sonar man screamed.

"Two torpedoes astern. Range five thousand meters, speed sixty miles per hour." He paused, then added, "Computer calculates they are Mk-48s."

Snapped from his daydream, the captain let the tea cup he was holding drop and smash on the floor. "Maximum revolutions," he bawled, "depth two hundred. I want the course plotted and countermeasures ready to launch. Weapons, work out firing solution for counter attack."

The submarine shuddered as the engines applied full power and began the age-old tactic of trying to outrun the incoming torpedo and get below the thermocline layer to confuse the incoming torpedoes' targeting systems. Watching the crew around him, the captain knew that in all probability it was too late. Five thousand meters was too close to run from and, even though they would try, all increasing speed and changing depth would do was add extra seconds to their lives. He could tell from looks he was receiving from his crew that they realized the harsh truth too. Their grim looks of determination showed that they would play the game to the end and maybe, just *maybe*, would win.

Being a submariner was normally a quiet and stealthy profession as you crept through the oceans using skill and guile to avoid detection. But not today as fifteen Chinese submarines suddenly started making enough noise to be heard by every listening device over the vast area of water as their propellers churned the water and launched electronic and noise countermeasures in vain attempts to escape death.

The American, Russian, and Canadian submarine captains were too experienced compared to their Chinese counterparts, who as a country did not have the same level of submarining training or heritage. They had spent days using every ounce of their skill to slowly maneuver themselves to be in the optimum position to strike.

In the Song-class submarine, the captain listened as a sailor called out the rapidly reducing distance of the approaching torpedoes. He had a momentary moment of hope as an explosion shook the hull when one of the torpedoes exploded as a decoy worked and tricked its targeting systems. It disappeared when the sonar operator shouted, the panic in his voice evident. "The second one has reacquired us. Distance five hundred meters."

He had time to turn to his second-in-command and shake his hand and say, before the warhead exploded in the stern of the submarine, "It has been an honor to serve with you." Their eyes locked in the tense seconds before the torpedo impacted.

Death came in an instant as the hull, massively compromised by the explosion, imploded and water under immense pressure filled the compartments, its force blowing open the watertight doors that were intended to separate them. An invisible wall of super compressed air, heated to hundreds of degrees Celsius, rushed ahead of the wall of water instantly incinerating everything in its path a fraction of a second before the water extinguished the brief but deadly fireball.

The hull sank rapidly into the unfathomable depths, screeching and groaning as the increasing pressure buckled and crushed it to an unrecognizable lump of scrap.

Only one submarine escaped this fate.

The sinking of the Chinese submarines was the signal for the ballistic missile subs to launch their payloads. Both US and Russian ballistic missile submarines launched Tomahawk and Kalibr cruise missiles respectively and they skimmed the ocean, honing their deadly payloads toward the Chinese.

Coordinating with these launches perfectly, the combined surface fleets of both navies surged forwards and launched a mass volley of more cruise and anti-ship missiles, which closely followed the first wave of ship killers streaking across the oceans to inundate the Chinese.

CHAPTER
TWENTY-FIVE

Major Benjamin Bowden looked out of the open rear loading ramp of the Hercules Transport aircraft he and the men of A squadron were in at the countryside passing not far below him. His preference would have been to do a high-altitude night drop, but the logistics of the whole operation meant daylight was crucial.

Both SAS squadrons, supported by over five hundred US Rangers, were in a fleet of planes flying a tree-top level circuitous route, dodging all major concentrations of Chinese forces, heading for the skies above Fort Deitrich. The original plan to HAHO parachute in had changed: as the mission planning progressed it was thought a night drop would be too risky, potentially scattering their forces over too wide an area to be effective. The men of the Special Air Service were all qualified jumpers, but not enough of the rangers were versed in the dangerous insertion method, which ruled it out entirely.

Another force was setting up refueling staging posts for the fleet of helicopters heading toward a location already secured by another smaller detachment of rangers in a remote forest clearing north of their target.

He was linked to the cockpit of the plane by a headset plugged into a port on the bulkhead behind him. When the captain informed him the drop zone was approaching he removed the headset and stood up, indicating to his men to get ready as the red light lit up on the rear bulkhead.

They all stood and shuffled toward the ramp. The jumpmaster secured to the plane by a strong umbilical cord stood at the edge of the ramp looking down at the ground rushing by.

Jumping without a static line was risky from the altitude they were at, but his men were superbly trained, and he could rely on them. The light changed to green and without hesitation Bowden took a few quick shuffling steps and leapt from the rear of the plane. It took a few seconds to stabilize from the buffeting of the airstream before he pulled the release handle on the parachute which streamed out of the pack on his back, fluttered for a few nervous seconds, and then filled with air, arresting his rapid descent. Quickly finding the control loops he looked down to choose his landing spot on the rapidly approaching ground.

Twenty seconds after leaving the Hercules, he pressed the release catch on his parachute, loosened the straps that held his weapon tightly to his chest, and raised his rifle searching for targets.

Looking around he could see the rest of his command doing similar. Not far away the skies were filled with other ballooning parachutes as the skilled pilots dropped their cargos over their predetermined drop locations.

Pulling a ruggedized tablet computer from a pouch he checked it as his men gathered in a defensive cordon around him. A squadron were the rescue squad and B squadron were to provide close support and extra manpower if needed. The rangers had been dropped at four points around the perimeter of the base and were tasked with being the first line of defense against any Chinese attack. This was thought highly likely as intelligence placed a sizeable force in the town that bordered the science facility.

His sergeant knelt next to him. "Which way, Ginge?"

He pointed to the remains of a building next to the clearing they had landed in. "For once, the flyboys got it right on the money and dropped us on top of it. It's that one."

The building, or what was left of it, was in a mess. The precision strike by China's new secret weapon had destroyed it and most of the others he could see. The walls and roof had partially collapsed, steel supports leaned at angles, and smoke rose from fires that had burned out but still smoldered.

"Where are the runners?" he asked. "Before we begin we need to make sure everyone is in position."

With the new and unknown capabilities of the Chinese radio-locating rocket system they had chosen to go old-school in their communication procedures. Runners had been selected from each unit who would be tasked with relaying information between the forces scattered around the base.

The sergeant called out and four men stepped forward, and after being shown where to go on the major's tablet they set off running. While they were waiting for them to return Bowden and his sergeant entered the building to see how big a task they faced.

Carefully climbing over and under fallen debris they worked their way deeper into the wreckage. The news was good and bad. They could see the access door and now understood why the scientists were trapped inside. Large sections of the steel roof structure had collapsed and were piled up against it.

The runners had returned by the time they had extricated themselves from the building. All the rangers were in position and digging in, awaiting the expected Chinese attack.

"Okay boys, shall we get on with it?" he started. "B squadron set up a perimeter. A squadron wait here until the demolition boys decide how many of us they'll need."

The explosive experts entered the ruined building and conducted a survey of the task ahead. One reported back quickly estimating it should take an hour or two to clear and stabilize the exit route for the trapped scientists and they would need a further twenty men to help shift the debris.

Major Bowden studied his watch. "The choppers should be here by then. Crack on, Sergeant."

Due to the black out on radio transmissions, the plan was for two Apache attack helicopters, that were already at the extraction point a twenty-minute flight time away, to fly to their location. If those on the ground were not fighting the Chinese the helicopters were to land and get further instructions, or if they were engaged to use their rockets and canons to assist. They were only to land if the pilots deemed it safe to do so. They would then report back and if they had been given the 'Go' by the SAS, would escort the transport helicopters back to the base to extract them.

Radios were only authorized to be used if there was no other option and the success or failure of the mission depended on it, making the potential risk of a salvo of missiles honing-in on their signal acceptable.

He ordered twenty men to be on standby to help those inside the building, then arrayed the rest around the building and got them busy preparing defensible positions. Soon cracks of explosions sounded from the building as steel beams and other debris were blasted clear.

A corporal near him was unpacking and preparing a small drone. It was a new addition to their equipment, and one that many other armed forces and government agencies were beginning to use, giving them the capability to quickly and easily gather intelligence and survey the area around them. The four rotors of the drone emitted a shrill whirr as it rose quickly and soared away. The corporal studied the screen on the small control console as the high-resolution camera sent back the live feed. Major Bowden ignored the temptation to see what was being displayed. He had a job to do and if anything was spotted he would be the first to find out.

Clearing the debris from the doorway was progressing. Cutting tools which would have made the job a lot easier are heavy, so they had been unable to bring anything but simple hand tools when parachuting in. Using their ingenuity, they were working their way through the mass of twisted and burnt metal using explosives to cut through beams and whatever they could find and use to prop up and stabilize places that needed it. The scientists knew they were coming and could most likely hear the efforts to rescue them. The major stood at the entrance to the building watching the soldiers clear the door area, nervously drumming his fingers against his leg.

A shout from the drone operator caused him to run over. "We have Chinese inbound," he stated and pointed to the screen. Armored vehicles supported by walking soldiers were advancing along the road toward the base.

"How far away are they?"

The operator turned a dial and the image zoomed out. "About half a mile I reckon. The Yanks are going to be busy soon."

He turned to the soldier by his side. "Jonesy, run over and warn them they have four APCs and approximately two hundred on foot heading their way. Tell them we will monitor from here and will reinforce if necessary."

Turning to look at the sky he spoke to no one in particular. "I hope those choppers turn up soon, we may have need of them before too long."

Even though lightly armed with only small arms, squad support weapons, and some anti-armor rocket launchers, the major knew they would fight with a rage and purpose that would defeat a far greater force.

The issue they faced was logistics—they only had the ammunition they carried when they parachuted in, with no chance of a resupply. If the Chinese attack was large and sustained there was the real and worrying possibility of running out.

Everything was going to plan. A Chinese attack was not unexpected, but time was the issue that weighed heavily on the mission. The rangers and the SAS needed to buy them enough time, fighting any counterattack while the extraction needed to be timed properly to avoid the defense getting overwhelmed by the attack.

The rattle of small arms fire and a few explosions began as the runner returned. The drone showed that the attack was only coming from one direction so Major Bowden ordered the runners to go to the defenders covering the three other sides of the base to tell them what was going on and to send a quarter of their men to bolster those engaging the enemy.

The drone was a useful asset enabling him to monitor the battle. The leading two armored personnel carriers had been hit by rocket fire and were burning fiercely. The rangers had stopped the Chinese advance dead, but from his overhead view he could see more troops working their way forward using covering fire provided by the heavy machine guns on the remaining APCs. Two troops of SAS were dispatched when a unit of Chinese soldiers were spotted detaching from the main attacking force and began to work their way around the perimeter fence. The drone followed their progress until they were cut down by a volley of fire from his men.

The advantage was in the hands of the attackers. Unable to hit the APCs who were firing from behind cover, the Chinese had reorganized after the initial shock of being attacked and were slowly advancing. The outcome was inevitable, but the aim was not to win but to buy enough time. Reports from the runners kept him up to date and from the overhead images he could see the Americans were doing an excellent job, slowly retreating from the advancing Chinese, making them pay dearly for every yard they gained.

There was no point telling the men working in the building to hurry up. They would be working as fast as the conditions allowed and they would also be able to hear the gunfire and know that the clock was ticking. Feeling rather than hearing the approaching helicopters as they disturbed the air around him, the major searched the skies until the sound of their rotor blades cutting the air filled the sky, followed moments later by them skimming low over the rooftops. One flared for landing as the other hovered overhead.

The pilot opened the window on the cockpit and the major approached, crouching under the downwash, and put on the headset the pilot passed to him, enabling them to communicate. They had a brief conversation before the pilot applied power and the helicopter jumped into the air and the two dipped their noses and sped toward the battle.

Soon the sounds of their chain guns firing and rockets exploding filled the air.

The corporal operating the drone kept everyone updated on the progress as the helicopters swung the battle once more in the favor of the defenders, destroying the two armored vehicles with Hellfire rockets and strafing the soldiers with machine gun fire and volleys of Hydra unguided missiles.

The major called to his men as a single Apache flew overhead. "One of the Apaches will remain on station; the other is going to lead the others in. ETA about forty minutes."

The corporal operating the drone shouted, "Tanks! Fucking loads of the buggers coming down the road. Looks like a lot of troop transport too."

"Shit," Bowden replied. "Corporal, are they approaching from anywhere else?"

"Not that I can see, boss. It looks as if they're only coming down the one road."

He turned to his runners who were standing near him. "Get all forces to the front gate. I want a fighting retreat back to here. Tell them we need one more hour. The Apache is good, but it will not be able to hold them back for long."

He called the major leading B squadron and the captains to gather around. "Go and support the Americans. We haven't got many AT4s," he said, meaning the shoulder-fired anti-tank launchers, "so I do not need to tell you to use them sparingly. We need to hold them off for as long as possible. If that armor breaks through we are going to be on a bit of a sticky wicket." He looked at his watch. "Thirty-five minutes gentlemen at least until the choppers get here. Good luck, chaps."

The men were ready to go and in minutes had run toward the sounds of firing. Bowden then turned and ran toward the building to help the men inside clear the last of the debris as the corporal shouted, "Helicopter's bloody hit, sir! Multiple anti-air missiles. It looks as if it got the lead tanks though. The other tanks have paused, but the soldiers are still advancing."

Inside the building the gunfire and crump of explosions was muted. The door was almost cleared—there was just one more steel beam to remove and the soldiers were calculating the best angle to apply their explosive charges. They feared if they overdid it, the rest of the roof that was precariously holding on above their heads may come crashing down.

Judging they had it right, everyone moved to a safe distance before detonating the explosive charge, which to their relief worked perfectly, and the last obstacle was cleared from the door. The roof above looked in danger of collapsing imminently though, and the few remaining supports swayed and creaked as they fought against the weight bearing down on them.

The code to override the door lock was committed to Bowden's memory and he inputted the eight-digit number into the keypad, watching with relief when the light changed to green and he could hear the internal mechanisms on the door releasing the bolts. The door pushed open as soon as it was unlocked, and a woman stepped out. She was wearing uniform with the insignia of a colonel on her shoulder boards.

Major Bowden saluted smartly, safely inside a windowless building and safe from any enemy snipers. "Good morning, Colonel. Major Benjamin Bowden of Her Majesties Armed Forces at your service. I believe you ordered a taxi? If you could gather your possessions it will be outside shortly."

She looked shocked. Shaking his hand, she introduced herself. "Colonel Mary Wordsmith. You're a Brit? The last communication we had before getting cut off was rescue was on its way. We could hear the explosions so knew something was up, but I never reckoned on being rescued by you lot. Anyway, you are here and that's all that matters."

"It's not just us, ma'am. There is a batta—" He stopped as bullets peppered the building, punching holes through the thin metal sheeting. More guns joined in and the volume increased.

A fight was raging just outside the door. Major Bowden turned to his men and ordered, "Get out there and see what's going on."

He turned back to the colonel. "If you could just wait here, please? I'd better check what on earth is going on. Some of them must have sneaked through the perimeter we are trying to maintain until the choppers get here. If you could get everyone inside ready to depart along with whatever stuff you need to bring, I'd be grateful."

As he turned away the colonel asked, "Do you need any of our boys? The two privates who were on guard duty when the bombs hit are down there." She waved her hand at the doorway behind her.

"I think we are going to need everyone who can fire a gun if we are going to get out of here. Send them up."

She called through the door and within seconds two men appeared both armed with rifles. They followed him as he strode toward the exit. Stopping at the doorway he crouched low and glanced out. His men were behind cover firing at a building across the open area.

He called to the captain nearest to him. "What's going on, Tony?"

"Not sure, Ginge. I think it's a small squad that somehow

broke through the perimeter. I don't think there are more than ten of them."

"What happened to the men watching that sector?"

"Unknown currently. There was some contact the other side of the building then we came under fire. I can only presume they have been overrun."

"Okay. We need to secure the landing zone. The choppers are going to be here soon. Lay down suppressing fire and I'll work around their flank."

He looked around and asked, "Where is the drone operator?"

"Over here, Ginge," called the corporal who was lying prone, using a small tree as tenuous protection. "It's gone. A round from one of the first volleys hit the control unit and buggered it up."

Bowden let out a string of curses, venting his frustration at losing such a vital piece of equipment. "Troops one and two on me. Let's get on with it and outflank these bastards. The rest of you keep their bloody heads down."

Outgoing fire grew as every soldier opened up on the building the Chinese were occupying. Waiting until the incoming fire died down, the major led the two troops to some buildings also badly damaged to their right. They quickly worked around the back of these, leapfrogging forwards.

Verbal communications were not necessary. Using hand signals the elite soldiers silently and quickly worked their way to a building adjacent to the one the Chinese had somehow reached. It was not as damaged as others having missed a direct hit from the bombs.

"Okay lads. You know what to do. Split into your patrols. One window each, don't fuck about with flashbangs this time. Chuck grenades in and standard CQB drill."

He grinned, loving the close quarters battle acronym and how the words made him feel. "Which one of you lucky bastards wants me with them?"

The men trained continuously together. As their commanding officer he still trained with the men, but not with a particular troop or the smaller patrols within them. He would therefore be an extra man attached to one of the established tightly knit groups of warriors along with the small contingent of headquarters personnel acting as his permanent shadow.

"Ginge," said one of the sergeants, "it would be an honor to babysit you. If you could keep the pointy end of your gun away from me and my mates I'd appreciate it though," he said using the time-honored joke of soldiers ridiculing the competence of their superior officers.

"Thank you, Chalky. I'll even let you buy the first round in the pub for that, you cheeky bastard. Right, come on lads. Choppers are inbound, let's get this over with."

The men split into their patrols and, crouching low, approached the building, each one gathering around a mostly glassless window. At a signal from the major two grenades were thrown through each. As soon as they exploded the men climbed through and entered the building. The Chinese, concussed by the grenades, did not stand a chance against such superbly trained soldiers who swept through the building, using speed and aggression; they killed everyone inside within thirty seconds.

After a second sweep though the rooms to ensure none had been missed, they gathered outside. The sounds of the battle were getting closer as the Chinese inexorably pushed the defenders slowly back.

"Well done, men. We can't have them sneaking up on us again. If you lot could stay here and watch this sector, I'll go and see how the others are doing. The recall signal will be my whistle."

Indicating four men to follow him he ran toward the ever-closing sounds of gunfire. He found the major in command of B squadron; he, along with his men, was protecting the right flank of the line of defenders.

"Ginge? How's it going back there?"

"Not too bad our end, Charlie. We've got the scientists out and the choppers should be here soon. We just had a little trouble with a few of our little friends sneaking up on us. Got a few of us I'm afraid before we dealt with them."

"Yeah, sorry. I thought a few got past us, but I couldn't send a runner, we were too heavily engaged. I can't spread the boys out any thinner or we won't hold the main force back. We have taken out their armor and they don't seem to want to send any more at us, but they are tough little buggers. There are just too many of them and to top it all off we are just about out of ammo."

Ben looked at an injured soldier being treated by another. "How many casualties?"

Charlie replied, his voice suddenly somber and full of emotion, "Three dead, five wounded and I don't think two of them will make it. These scientists better be able to do what they bloody promised for the price my lads have paid."

Ben nodded his head sadly in agreement as he briefly thought how many more letters he would need to write to wives or mothers before they were safely back in Canada. He slapped Charlie on the back.

"Come on mate, there's still plenty of fight left in our boys. It won't be long now. I'll get your wounded back to the extraction point and get ready for the recall. I think when I call it, it's going to get a little… *interesting* around here. I'm going to check on the rangers and then gather up the wounded."

It took him a few minutes to find the colonel in charge of the rangers. His story was no different to Charlie's. His men had fought above and beyond his expectations, repulsing attack after attack by hugely numerically superior forces. They had made the Chinese pay dearly for every inch of ground they had yielded to them but at a heavy cost to themselves.

His depleted forces were low on ammunition but not low on

courage, stating they would fight them with rocks and fists before they let them get any closer. Ginge told him to start getting his own wounded back as they would be the first on the helicopters after the scientists. And to start planning and preparing for a rapid fall back when the order came.

Each carrying or helping a wounded man, Ginge and the men with him ran the few hundred yards back to their original location. The scientists were gathered outside, crouching behind any cover they could find, each carrying bags or rigid cases containing the materials and documents they would need to continue their work.

"Why aren't you inside, Colonel?" he asked the lead scientist. "The building will at least offer you some protection. I cannot guarantee your safety as it is."

"Major, I understand, but I asked your men to set explosives inside the lab. The materials and research it contains cannot fall into Chinese hands. They are doing it now and are concerned the building will collapse when the charges go off. So here we are."

He looked at the building. "Okay. Just stay down and do what I or any of my men tell you."

Three soldiers ran from the building shouting for everyone to clear the area. Seconds later the ground shook and a fireball boiled through the ruined roof of the building. It proved too much for its tenuous defiance of gravity and it collapsed, the remains of its walls falling in on itself.

He glanced at the captain who had led the demolition team.

He was smiling, reveling in the destruction he had caused. Seeing the look on his commanding officer's face, he intoned, "They don't pay us to bring it back, Ginge."

Shaking his head, Ginge replied, "Bloody idiots, the lot of you. Right then, you three have just earned the privilege of collecting half of everyone's remaining ammunition and distributing to those on the perimeter."

The captain lifted a bag he was carrying. "I took the liberty of clearing out the arms locker in the guard room of the lab before we blew it up, Ginge. There was a fair few mags of .556 and a 9 mil pistol in it, so I thought it may come in useful."

He smiled at the captain this time. "Bertie, you are forgiven. Get some of it to the Yanks too. They are running as low as our lads are."

The three men went around the few remaining members of the squadron guarding the extraction point and took spare magazines from them, stuffing them in to the bags that had contained the explosives before running off toward the sounds of firing which was building in intensity as the defenders gave their all to hold the line.

They waited.

Five tense minutes later the air once again reverberated with the sound of helicopters approaching fast. The Apache roared low overhead and circled the extraction site. Ginge ran into the open waving his arms to get the attention of the pilot. Using basic communication by waving his arms around he conveyed the mission was successful and for him to support the soldiers on the perimeter. Giving the thumbs up the pilot banked the helicopter steeply and seconds later the sounds of its chain gun firing and rockets exploding rose above the continuous clattering of small arms fire. Seconds later the distinctive heavy *whop-whop-whop* of Chinooks approaching cut through the air as three of the large twin rotor helicopters swooped in low and landed quickly and heavily.

The four Blackhawk helicopters that had been flanking them remained hovering overhead, their door gunners firing toward the attackers. Spent bullet casings poured from the sky as a solid stream of heavy lead was sent toward them. Running toward the scientists he got a few of them to help the wounded soldiers. Dragging the slower ones, he and his men quickly got them all on board and gave the signal to take off as he stepped off the ramp.

Buffeted by the downwash he watched as it sped away over the ruined base, the crewman operating the rear gun blazing away in the direction of the Chinese.

He stood, listening to the continuous roar of battle, trying to judge from the noise how it was progressing.

Right then, he thought. *Mission accomplished. We are fighting for ourselves now.*

He turned to the runners. "Hopefully the choppers will give us the breathing space we need to pull back. Go and tell them to start extricating themselves. We will hold the inner perimeter to cover them. This is going to be a close-run thing so tell 'em no fucking about or they may get left behind."

Positioning themselves in a cordon around the helicopters he and his men placed spare magazines within easy reach and prepared themselves for what they fully expected to be a desperate few minutes.

Within minutes the first rangers appeared. They were the walking wounded, some helping each other they staggered bloody, battered, and filthy toward the waiting helicopters. Some Ginge noticed had their main weapons slung and were holding their sidearms in their hands showing they had expended all their ammunition and were down to holding back the advancing horde with only pistol rounds.

The next Chinook, filled to above normal operating capacity, applied full power and slowly heaved itself into the sky with its guns firing. Ginge looked back with relief when one Sea King and two Sikorsky Cyclone helicopters flew in low and landed hard. They must have been loitering nearby, waiting for the first few Chinooks to depart before committing themselves.

The Chinooks and Blackhawks he knew would not have had the capacity to take them all, with the new arrivals he knew they would have. If they were still alive, that was.

The next rangers to stagger past were each burdened by the weight of one of their comrades carried over their shoulders. From the way their arms and legs hung limp, it was clear they were their dead. Leaving them behind to not be honored and buried was never an option and they would take priority over the living.

Next in small groups came the men still capable of fighting, most bleeding or limping they filed onboard the waiting helicopters which lifted off as soon as they could fit in no more.

The colonel was the last to appear. His face bleeding and his arm supported by a makeshift sling he stopped, told the men with him to get to one of the helicopters and crouched down next to Ginge.

"It's just your boys now. The helos are just about holding them back, but they must know we are pulling out. Soon there is going to be a shit-ton of them heading our way when they realize there ain't anyone firing back."

Ginge raised the whistle that hung from a lanyard around his neck. "Get yourself on a chopper, Colonel. As soon as I blow this whistle my lads will be running faster than Usain Bolt with the shits for last lift out of here." There was something in the way he had said it that made the colonel look at him.

"And what about you?"

He shrugged. "I've got myself a nice spot here. I figure the Chinese will come racing around that corner over there soon. I'm reckoning I can bag myself a brace of two of them and buy the lads some time to get away."

He was offering to sacrifice his own life to give his men enough time to get away. The colonel kneeled next to him behind the pile of rubble, using it as a makeshift firing position. "You have indeed got a nice spot here. Would you mind if you had some company?"

Both knowing what they were resigning themselves to do, he said nothing but nodded. The colonel eased his blood-covered arm from the sling and checked his rifle was loaded, then placed his last two remaining magazines beside the ones Ginge had put within easy reach.

"Ready when you are, Major."

Ginge raised the whistle to his lips and blew a long series of short, sharp shrill blasts. More whistles sounded as his captains responded, blowing blasts of their own.

Men rose from their positions, running hell for leather back toward the waiting helicopters. As one filled and rose into the air, one of the Blackhawks hovering overhead firing at the attackers descended to take its place. The pilots must have decided to risk using the radios to communicate with each other as it was so well choreographed.

The last man to pass their position was one of his captains who, on seeing his commanding officer and the American colonel together, skidded to a halt.

"Come on, Ginge," he shouted.

"Smithy, get on the chopper." He indicated upwards. "We'll hold them off and get the next lift."

He looked at him and the colonel next to him with a worried look on his face. "Sir?"

Giving the captain an apologetic half grin, he replied, "Don't you look at me in that tone of voice, Smithy. Someone needs to do this, and I will not ask it of anyone else, so that's the end of it. Now be a good chap and give me any spare mags you have then kindly fuck off and get on the chopper."

The colonel fired at a group of Chinese who had rounded the corner, stopping any more debate or protests the captain might have tried. They dived back behind cover leaving two of their number lying on the ground.

Reaching into his pouch he pulled out two magazines and handed them to Ginge. He then stood to attention, gave a smart salute to his major and said, "It's been an honor," before turning and running full pelt to the last chopper on the ground.

"Piss off," Ginge replied with a laugh and shouted at his receding back, "try again without the melodrama?"

Smithy shouted back as he ran and tried something a little more British, "Don't go being a wanker."

"I wouldn't give them the satisfaction," Ginge yelled back over the sound of gunfire. "Now, off you fuck!"

Before Smithy reached the helicopter, the Chinese came

around the corner in strength. Picking their shots carefully the two men fought side by side, bullets striking all around them as the attackers soon discovered their position and directed all their fire toward them.

Hearing the engine noise on the helicopter change as it began to take off, both men switched their weapons to fully auto and emptied their rifles at the Chinese. A final short burst of cannon fire from the Apache blew apart a larger group that rushed into view before it peeled away and followed the Blackhawk. Flinching involuntarily from the incoming fire that hit all around them they fought their last stand. Surrender never entered their minds, both knew they would keep fighting while they had breath in their body.

Bleeding from dozens of wounds caused by razor-sharp brick splinters and other shrapnel that continually swept over them, they kept firing, bodies mounting as they beat off attack after attack. The colonel threw his rifle down as he fired his last bullet and pulled out his pistol. Ginge did the same when he emptied his last magazine at a group who were trying to outflank their position.

For the first time, the incoming fire made them duck down and take cover. Ginge looked at the colonel and said, "Well that was fun whilst it lasted. One more time, Old Boy?"

"Sure, son," he said with resigned satisfaction. "This sure has been one hell of a fight. As the ranking officer here, I could order you to try and make a break for it. But I think, my friend, I'd be wasting my time."

"That you would, sir," Ginge said, "that you bloody would."

In between lulls in firing, Chinese voices could be heard shouting commands. You didn't need to understand the language to know it was the officers urging their men forward for one final assault.

Ginge reached into his backpack that lay open by his side and picked up his last grenade, pulling the pin as he held it in his hand.

"Ready?" he asked. Not waiting for the reply, he threw it over the battered and much reduced wall of rubble.

As soon as the grenade exploded, they jumped to their feet, pistols held out ready in front of them, searching for targets. After firing off only two shots each, they were both knocked off their feet by the blast wave of an explosion directly in front of them. Debris rained down on top of them as they lay there, senses dulled by the shock until another explosion, this time slightly further away followed by a sound they both knew well made them gain their feet and stare forwards.

The area that seconds before had been filled with Chinese soldiers was empty of the living. Bodies lay scattered from the force of the explosion. Thirty-millimeter cannon fire ripped into the ground destroying anything it touched.

It could only be coming from an Apache; nothing else they had had that sort of fire power. The noise of another helicopter approaching made them turn around. One of the Blackhawks was approaching. Flying low and crabbing in sideways, its door gunner firing over their heads.

They did not need telling twice to run toward the rapidly descending helicopter, both diving in before it touched down. They clung on as the pilot expertly turned and at high speed raced at ground level through the base using the ruined buildings as cover before eventually gaining altitude, and raced away across the Maryland countryside. Getting to his knees on the hard floor Ginge was helped into a seat by his grinning captain nicknamed Smithy. He was handed a headset so they could communicate.

"Thank you, Smithy, but when I told you to fuck off, I meant *all* the way off and not to embark on some bloody half-arsed rescue mission."

"Well, boss, there's no way we could allow the Victoria Cross you will probably get to be posthumous. As you well know the penalty for getting one is unlimited drinks in the mess for those involved in the action and managed not do anything as stupid as get a medal. Also, the Yanks were not keen about leaving their colonel behind, so we had a little chat and decided to swing on by and see if we could get your backsides out of the pickle you got yourselves in."

Ginge smiled at the loyalty his men had shown to him. His face then dropped theatrically when he thought about what Smithy had said about the fine he would pay if for some reason they decided his actions deserved a medal.

"On seconds thoughts, Smithy," he said, "can you drop me back please? I can't afford to buy you buggers that many drinks."

CHAPTER
TWENTY-SIX

TEXAS

"Madam President, we have received a message. The scientists have been rescued," Sebastian informed her as she sat at the large table in the central room of the ranch in Texas that, for the last forty-eight hours, had been the seat of government for the United States.

Communication was still restricted to Morse code; they used a hastily developed system of code words made up of slang or oblique references they hoped would, in the short term, outwit any Chinese intercepts.

Despite their pleas, wanting her to be whisked out of the country to avoid any possibility of her falling into Chinese hands again, she was insistent that she would never do that. Following a brief communication with her husband, Steve, who was at the Holly River Base she'd ordered plans be drawn up to get her there where they could establish a permanent base of resistance.

"That's good news, Sebastian. Has Fen Shu divulged any useful information yet?"

"Not yet, ma'am. She is proving very difficult to get any sense out of at all. I'm no expert, but I think she has had a complete mental breakdown now that all her plans have come off the rails. No matter what I have tried, and trust me, apart from pulling her fingernails out I have used every technique I know. If I could get hold of a few vials of drugs that I know will loosen her tongue, I may have a chance.

"She has periods of lucidity where she is back to her usual vicious self and then she loses it, wailing on about a lost brother and how she let him down and wants to make it right again. I honestly do not know what she is on about. I have checked, and General Liu does not know anything about a brother. As far as he knows, she is the only child of the brother of the president, always living in the privileged, cosseted world of the top-level inner circles of the government.

"If she had a brother, in the misogynistic Chinese culture, he would surely have taken precedence over a mere woman. Even the mentally challenged idiot offspring of senior government officials manage to get high profile cushy jobs of one sort or another. They just have a team of underlings employed to do the job for them."

"Maybe she needs a woman's touch, Sebastian? A gentler approach after the treatment she has received and what she has gone through in the last few days. Let me have a talk with her."

"I'm all out of ideas, so it's worth a try certainly, Madam President."

"Okay, so tell me all she has told you about this brother. And please can you call me Madeline? I'm finding all this formality a little irksome considering the situation we are in."

Sebastian stood awkwardly for a few moments before responding, "I don't think I can do that, Madam President. It just wouldn't be right for me to address you less formally. Things may not be as they should, but you are still the president and represent all that it stands for. What else are we fighting for if not the United States of America? And you, through no design or fault of your own, are our leader."

"Okay, Sebastian. I understand. Thank you for your unquestioning loyalty and patriotism. But can you promise me one thing, when this is all over and we find ourselves sharing a bottle of bourbon, sitting in some comfortable chairs in front of a blazing fire, I order you to call me Madeline."

He smiled and nodded his head. "Yes, Madam President, I can see that would be the occasion to drop the formalities. Now, let me tell you all that she had me about this brother."

Madeline walked down the steep stairs that led to the basement and asked the guard to unlock the door.

Fen Shu was locked in a windowless dusty storeroom in the cellar. She was shackled by her arms and legs to a length of chain padlocked to a fixing bolted to the rough stone wall.

Kept in total darkness to disorientate her, her chains clinked and hampered her attempts to shield her eyes with her arm when the door was opened and the single light bulb hanging from the ceiling was turned on.

The cellar was cool and smelled musty from disuse. It had most likely been designed as a cold store for storing foodstuffs and had become redundant over time as refrigeration replaced its need.

There were no comforts in the room. A blanket lay on the bare earth floor and a single bucket was in a corner for her toilet needs. This had been knocked over and its contents created a stinking damp patch on the dusty floor.

Fen Shu, her face dirty and streaked with tears, screamed, "Get me a new bucket, I cannot see it in the dark. Send someone in to tidy it *now!*"

Her eyes looked wild and her face, which had usually been a mask of calm and confidence, now looked scared, desperate, and more than a little unhinged.

Madeline studied her. Sebastian's summary looked accurate. Her composed and confident outer shell had been stripped away. She was going to be the person who delivered America to her country, and she probably thought that they would still be successful, but she herself had failed, allowing not only for the president to escape but for herself to be captured.

Failure in her country was not an option. Even her uncle would not be able to save her from the disgrace that had befallen her. The only power she held now was the location of the virus antidote. Her warped mind, twisted further beyond the realms of reality, believed she could use the information to turn the tables on her captors, recapture the president, and return in triumph to continue her mission and wipe out the shame she felt.

"GET OUT, you *bitch*!" she screamed when she recognized Madeline. "I will not tell you *anything*. That pathetic man you sent could not get me to talk and you will not either. I demand better quarters," she screeched petulantly. "You will all pay for this when this puny rebellion of yours gets crushed."

Madeline stood her ground, wanting nothing more than to silence her with a chair to the face. She could have vented once again the anger she felt toward this woman who was responsible for the deaths of millions, and the millions more who were dying slowly from the virus. Instead, she spoke softly. "No Fen Shu, I am not here to question you, but to ask for your help. I have had contact from some who have the most wonderful news for you."

"There is nothing I want from you. The only news I want is that your country is defeated, and you are offering me your surrender."

"You're probably right." Madeline looked over her shoulder theatrically as if to check they were not being overheard and lowered her voice. "I shouldn't tell you this, but you are winning. Every uprising has been crushed by your soldiers. It is only a matter of time before we too are captured."

She could see hope building in her. It was now time to deliver the lie. "But that is not why I am here. Your brother has been found in one of your camps. He identified himself to someone with the Red Cross who was doing an inspection. He had tried to tell your soldiers, but they did not believe him."

Madeline watched her face. Anyone with a sound mind would have questioned the story's validity, but it hit a spot in Fen's brain that wanted it to be the truth so very much that it subconsciously countermanded any doubts.

Her faced changed from shock to hope to happiness in a few seconds. Tears of joy ran down her face. "Where is he? I must go to him immediately."

"I will have to see if that is possible. Maybe we can have him brought to you here? But he is a long distance from here and with the country at war it could be difficult."

Fen though for a few seconds. "I can get him. I have full authority to travel anywhere and to use whatever resources are available."

Madeline held her hands up to silence her. "The problem is, we have learned that he is desperately ill from the virus. He may be too ill to travel." She let the statement hang in the air like a lure. Fen's current mental state made it easy to lead her on. She looked at Madeline, unable to separate truth from fiction, and she believed her.

She calculated that if they were soon to be overrun by Chinese forces, then it was irrelevant if they got hold of some of the antidote. It did not matter how it got there, through her own people or through the Americans. As she did not know when her people would come for her, the best chance for her brother would be to tell them where it was and let them get it to him.

"I can get the antidote for him. I cannot let him die, I must take care of him."

"Fen Shu," Madeline said kindly, "I know you've been asked many times where the antidote is being stored, but now I'm asking as one woman to another: please tell me where it is so I can get it to your brother before it's too late. If it was my brother or sister who was ill, who was *dying*, I would do *anything* to save them."

All sense and reasoning had left her. The lie, told so simply, had been accepted by her confused mind. "Get me a map of San Antonio. I can show you."

Everyone had been briefed about what was going on and how to act if the Chinese woman came into the room. She was to be treated with respect as it may further lower her defenses and stop her seeing through the lies she had been told. The men and women around the table nodded at her and moved respectfully out of the way as she was shown a large-scale map of San Antonio.

Fen took a minute to interpret the map and then pointed at

an area. "They are stored in the refrigerated area of the hospital morgue," she admitted.

"Thank you, Agent Shu," Tanner said as she tried not to crow with victory. "How many doses are stored there?"

"There are many thousands," Fen Shu said, "but that does not matter; you only need one for my brother."

Madeline glanced at Sebastian who was looking at the map. He turned and had a quiet conversation with some others before looking at Madeline and, nodding his head, gave her the thumbs-up. That was the signal she was looking for. They knew where the antidotes were and reckoned they could get them.

The look on Madeline's face changed from one of sympathetic understanding to one of pure venom and hatred. She turned to Fen Shu and slapped her hard around the face. Two men who had been standing ready stepped forward and grabbed her arms as she reeled from the shock of being hit.

"Did you really think we had found your brother?" she spat. "If we had, though, and if he was infected, I can personally guarantee you would have met him. You would be tied to a chair with your eyes glued open, so you did not miss a second of the suffering he would be going through. You would sit there and watch him die and then maybe, just maybe, you'd realize what thousands of Americans are doing right now as their children and loved ones lie dying from what you have released." She leaned back away from the horrified Chinese woman.

"And anyway," she went on in a calmer voice, "you better hope you are telling me the truth. That blanket you are sitting on in your stinking hole of a cell came from one of the camps. I think you will be the first person we test the antidote on, just to make sure it isn't another lie."

Fen Shu slowly began to comprehend that she had been duped. Fear spread over her face at the thought she had been in touch with a contaminated blanket, and then it dawned on her. She had been lied to about her brother. They had not found him. He wasn't ill. In fact, they didn't even know if he was alive at all.

She flew into a rage. The men could barely hold her as she fought against them, kicking and screaming like a possessed cat caught by animal control. She bucked and reared like a wild animal, snapping her teeth at the men struggling to restrain her as they tried to get her on the ground and reattach the shackles that had bound her hands and legs. When she was secured, Madeline crouched down and stared into her face that was contorted with the madness running through her brain.

"Did you really think you were going to win? We will destroy everyone that has tried to take our country from us."

She laughed in her face. Fen Shu stopped struggling and spat at the president with a look of hateful satisfaction at her empty gesture. Madeline leaned away with her eyes closed as she produced a handkerchief from a pocket to wipe away the spittle.

"Don't worry," she crooned menacingly, "I plan to keep you

alive long enough to witness the utter ruin that will befall your pathetic nation. The shame you will feel, knowing it is all your fault as your country falls apart is something I cannot begin to imagine. Take her back to her cell please, gentlemen."

She deliberately turned her back as Fen Shu was dragged away.

Sebastian approached her. "That was excellent work, Madam President. We're just finishing off the plans for attacking the missile command center and then we will get straight on to the best way to retrieve the antidotes."

"As she was talking, Sebastian, I could not help but think she could still be of use to us. She has the authority to go wherever she wants. We have General Liu's car, why don't we just try and use it and con our way in? Why fight our way in when we could just walk straight through the front door?"

Sebastian looked shocked at the simplicity of the plan. He thought for a few seconds and then smiled. "And you tell me you are no military leader, ma'am? That plan is genius, but I think it would be hard to get her to comply. Why don't we see if the general will help us? Sergeant Cho has already told us they had no problem getting through the roadblocks when he fled the city. I imagine in the chaos we caused getting you out, the news of the general's arrest will hopefully not have been widely broadcast."

He paused to give it more thought. "With just the two of them, we are risking little," he said. "They could be ready to go immediately. Can I suggest we both go and have a word with the general?"

CHAPTER
TWENTY-SEVEN

Marissa stood along with all the women and children she had been incarcerated with in the inner yard of the prison. They had woken up to find all the guards had disappeared overnight. Unsure of what to do they had waited. Unable to see over the walls, they had no idea what was happening. Rumors ran through the group of terrified women like wildfire. When the firing had first been heard in the distance, they all panicked and, fearing they may be attacked, sought places to hide. After hours with nothing happening, they slowly reemerged and gathered together.

Braving the wrath of guards they fully expected to appear again at any minute, they banged on the high steel main gates of the prison, attempting to get the attention of anyone, but to no avail. They were trapped in a prison that by design made it impossible, without any equipment or tools, to escape from.

Weak from the terrible diet and conditions they were forced to endure, with most of them worried and fearful for their loved ones they had forcibly separated from, the general mood was of helplessness and despondency. Marissa had luckily escaped what some of the women had endured. The younger, prettier ones had often been dragged screaming from the others. A few brave women, including Marissa, had been beaten when they tried to intervene.

Most of them returned hours later, beaten and broken from their ordeal. Some, ominously, did not. The commander of the camp took great delight in continually informing them in broken English they were now the possessions of the army of the People's Republic of China, and as such should be proud to be able to offer themselves as recreational items to the conquering, victorious soldiers.

Two women who had, at the beginning, fought against their captors so viciously and desperately that one soldier was killed, had been made an example of. They were forced to watch as the two women were brutalized and beaten by a mob of willing Chinese soldiers. More dead than alive, they were then hung from some hastily erected gallows and left as a reminder of what the price of non-cooperation was.

Suicide had unfortunately become commonplace, as some, unable to cope with what they were being forced to do, chose to end their own lives rather than allow themselves to be used in such a cruel and barbaric fashion.

Toby and Harris, escorted by Captain Troy and four of his

soldiers, approached the gates in the high climb-proof mesh outer fence of the prison. They had studied the place from cover nearby until they were satisfied that it too had been abandoned by the Chinese.

The other soldiers, without being ordered, spread out in a defensive cordon around them.

The gate was secured by a padlock which yielded easily to the bolt croppers Troy took from his pack. With the escorting soldiers scanning everywhere through the sights of their rifles they cautiously approached and inspected the main gate. It was made from solid steel with no visible locking mechanism.

Troy turned to one of the soldiers and pointed to the gate. "Dillon, if you wouldn't mind, please."

Dillon nodded and approached the gate, slinging his rifle over his shoulder as he ran his hands across its smooth surface. "No problem, sir. I'll have that open in no time. Couple of charges in the right place should crack it open."

Shrugging out of his pack he reached inside and retrieved the last few blocks of high explosives he had been carrying since they had resupplied at White Sulphur Springs. Troy walked back a safe distance.

Dillon attached, placed, and molded the soft compound around several places on the gate and inserted the detonators. Trailing wires from them he indicated for everyone to stand clear.

As soon as everyone moved to the side and pressed themselves against the high walls of the prison, he pressed the button on the box he held in his hand. The crack of explosives detonating was followed by the screeching and groaning of stressed metal, and one leaf of the gate slowly sagged forwards and came crashing down raising a cloud of dust.

"Good job, Dillon," said Troy as he slapped him on the back. Indicating for Toby and Harris to hang back he led the men through the dust and smoke and entered the prison.

The women inside were completely unaware of what was happening until the sharp crack of the explosives shocked them into activity. Screaming and shouting from the fright, they all ran to the far end of the yard and cowered staring into the impenetrable dust and smoke cloud that had been thrown up. Mothers covered their children with their own bodies. Marissa crouched near the front of the group, her arm protectively over a few near-hysterical women.

"Someone's coming. RUN!" screamed a voice as Marissa saw figures emerging through the dust cloud.

A figure in uniform, his face hidden behind his raised weapon approached, his rifle pointing all around as he scanned for threats. More figures silently emerged behind him.

"Marissa!" called a voice. Marissa's head snapped up, her mind trying to work out if she had really heard her name being called. Another voice began calling her name, a voice she recognized.

It couldn't be, though. They had never been far from her mind, but knowing her position was hopeless, she had given up all hope of ever seeing them again.

"Toby?" she shouted, raising herself up, her eyes searching everywhere.

Through the settling dust she made out the shapes of two more figures, this time running in her direction. She began sobbing uncontrollably as they ran into her embrace, her legs giving way as she knew her ordeal was over.

Emotions changed from fear to elation as they saw the faces of the soldiers were not Asian, but Caucasian, black, and Hispanic. And the badges on their arms were not the hated red with gold stars of their imprisoners and torturers but the stars and stripes of the country they had thought was no more.

As one they surged forwards and mobbed the men, every single one of them wanting to touch or have contact with their saviors. It took some time for calm to be restored and for Troy to be able to talk to the women.

He gave them a frank update on the wider news about how the resistance movements were beginning to get organized. Knowing that the president had been released, and how, and that other nations were helping gave everyone a psychological boost. As a country they were not alone. The propaganda continually broadcast through loud speakers telling them that as a nation they were defeated, and all other countries were quaking in fear of Chinese power and refusing to get involved had always been treated with suspicion, but as time passed, they could not deny that there must be an element of truth to them.

Why else would they be treated as they were? If China had any fear of reprisal, they would never be acting with the callous impunity they were. As Troy talked, he could see hope building up once again in the faces of the women.

He gave them two choices. They could make their way to the towns and villages they knew were clear of Chinese forces where they would be made welcome and accommodated the best they could, or they could return to their base at Holly River. He made no bones about the rough conditions at the camp, but he promised them security and safety there.

Most of the women were locals. Knowing now that their husbands possibly had been in the other camp and could be amongst those who escaped, they did not want to leave, but go and try to find them. They knew they could not return to Caldwell itself, but if they remained in the local area, then there was a chance they would be reunited.

Leaders emerged from amongst them and they began organizing the women into groups. All the local women wanted to stay and go to the nearest Chinese free areas. Those whose husbands might still be alive chose to stay, whereas the others decided to return to Holly River with Troy and his men.

Troy asked for volunteers from amongst his men to stay with the first group and escort them to their destination. They all volunteered so he ended up picking them himself. Marissa obviously wanted to go wherever Harris and Toby were going. She had no idea if any of her family was still alive and she had no way of reaching them. Toby had told her of their plan to get to his uncle, Fat Joe, in California. They had both promised her they would never let her out of their sight again and insisted that when they had gained their strength, they would begin their journey west.

He sent a runner to recall the soldiers he had dispatched to keep an eye on Caldwell. They reported very little activity. Patrols had restarted after they had shot and killed the two men they had witnessed entering the town. They had been forced to watch impotently, as again the same patrols found the latest escapees from the camp. As before no quarter was given and they had been annihilated by the Chinese.

Troy desperately wanted to organize an attack on the base. He knew that with the force he had with him now, even though they would not be able to destroy it, they could perform enough mischief to force the Chinese to keep on lock down as they were and dissuade them from venturing further afield.

Reluctantly he knew it would have to wait for another day. His priority was to those they had freed, to ensure they got somewhere safe. There was little point in delaying further. He had a final word with the men who were staying to escort the locals.

They had studied maps and worked out the best routes to take across the heavily forested hills and valleys, avoiding areas of population until they knew they were in a 'free' zone. His soldiers were instructed to make sure the women and children were safe and being cared for before making their own way back to the base, gathering intelligence and only attacking enemy forces if they could guarantee complete success. The last thing they would want is a pursuing force of Chinese endangering any civilians or following their trail back to the base.

Troy led half his men and thirty women and children through the woods to where they had hidden the trucks. Harris and Marissa supported Toby between them and they all set off back to Holly River.

Sitting in the lead truck Troy noticed many more vehicles, including a yellow school bus with Chinese markings stenciled on it, had arrived in his absence.

"It looks as if some of the militias have arrived," he said to the sergeant driving. "If you let me out here, can you see to the passengers please."

As he stepped from the truck a man stared at him, detached himself from the group he was talking to, and approached. Recognition flashed across Troy's face. It was the Englishman he had sent into Caldwell. He held out his hand and both smiling they shook hands. "Mister Calhoun, I never thought I'd get the chance see you again and thank you for all you did. The intel you sent was invaluable."

"It was nothing," Cal said in his self-effacing British manner. "It was the least I could do, those bastards needed to pay for killing Louise." He swallowed, pushing back down the lump in his throat. "They told me you'd be back soon after you had persuaded them to let you return to the camp. Tell me, how was it?"

"The men's camp was empty apart from two who stayed. They remembered you. You gave one of them some peanut butter. They reckon you saved his life. We did, though, free the women from the prison. Some of them have come back with us."

"Ah yes, I remember them. They were asking about a friend of theirs. Melanie or something?"

"Marissa is her name and if you go to the trucks, they should all be getting out now. Anyway, how the hell did you end up here?"

"Long story. The short version is I was on my way home, being driven in that yellow bus over there to a port where a ship was waiting, when the missiles started flying overhead and our guards ran away. I decided that it would be safer to try and find you, so we turned around and headed here. We almost got shot up by Reverend Harris and the Appalachian militia—the fact I mentioned your name helped them believe our story. They let us join them and led us the rest of the way. And so here I am."

"Well I'm glad you are here too. Now if you would excuse me I need to report to the senator and then I believe we are having a war council."

"I know, I'm invited too. A fellow Brit and I have volunteered to join up."

Troy smiled broadly and slapped him hard on the back. "We'd be glad to have you." He then turned and walked toward the cabin.

Cal looked at the trucks and recognized the big man who was helping another much thinner man from the back of one. A woman stood next to them, assisting as she too helped him climb down. He walked over to them.

"Hello," he said. "I'm glad you are okay; do you remember me?"

Harris and Toby both looked at him, recognizing him immediately. Toby shook his hand. "You're that British dude who helped me in the camp. How could I forget you, I reckon you saved my life, risking giving me the peanut butter. Thank you, man, thank you."

Cal turned to Marissa. "Troy tells me you were the one they asked me to help find. I'm sorry I couldn't do more, but they evacuated me before I could search the database we were building up."

Marissa gave Cal a hug. "It doesn't matter. I don't think it would have done any good anyway. The bastards were not interested in cataloguing the women; they treated us as disposable goods, not interested in who we were or where we came from. Toby and Harris told me about the kind Englishman who gave him some food. For that one act of kindness you have my eternal thanks."

Gordon approached and Cal introduced him and explained how they had met. Handshakes were exchanged all round and Gordon's upper-crust charm and mannerisms soon had the Americans laughing.

He pointed to a pile of camping gear that had been requisitioned from a local outdoor supplies shop. "Anyway, my first official job as the British Ambassador to the American resistance is to allocate suitable accommodation to the latest arrivals. As you all know each other could I suggest you get yourselves a suitable tent sorted and get it pitched. Make sure it has room for me too, please," he said as he began to walk off.

Cal called him back. "Er, Gordon… ambassador?"

"Yes, my dear chap. Made it up myself." He then whispered theatrically, "The Yanks seem to expect an English gentleman with a posh accent to have some sort of title. Ambassador suits me, I think. If I say it often enough it may stick."

Chapter Twenty-Eight

The English Channel

The Royal Navy deployed every vessel it had available to patrol the coastal waters around mainland Britain. The situation in mainland Europe was deteriorating by the day: food supplies ran out, and oil and gas shortages paralyzed the infrastructure that relied upon millions of gallons and cubic meters of oil and gas being imported daily.

Vast areas began experiencing blackouts which grew longer each day as power grids were stretched to their limit. Nuclear, coal, and alternative energy producers such as wind, tidal, and solar could not meet the demand gap as traditional power stations stopped generating when fuel supplies ran out. Some countries which had invested more heavily in alternative energy sources fared better, but still demand outstripped the available supply and Europe slowly went dark.

All other European countries had been unable to stop the riots and general disorder that overwhelmed the police and other emergency services. One by one they fell to chaos and anarchy, their governments powerless to stop it. Millions of people began to migrate either to escape the violence or search for rapidly dwindling food supplies.

Armed forces had been mobilized, but no government had the will to use them against their own citizens. Borders were also too long and wide open to stop the floods of refugees, who if stopped and turned back just tried again at another location. Emergency summits were held between all nations, but not one had the solution to the problems they were facing.

Curfews were announced but ignored, or became impossible to reinforce, as police officers stopped reporting for duty and mass desertions occurred across all areas of the military. The general feeling in most countries was the government was proving incapable of doing anything to help, so it was up to you to look after yourself and your family.

No one headed east toward Russia. They too had locked their border down hard, not in fear of refugees, but as part of the war footing the entire country had been put under. Their border guards, not shackled by any humanitarian designs, ensured no one entered their country. They had simple and clear instructions. One warning shout followed by one warning shot, then if their orders were not followed, they were authorized to use, without any further validation, deadly force.

The United Kingdom had chosen to play the field carefully; their own domestic situation had resolved itself dramatically after appeals from the leaders of all government parties had worked. The Russian oil and gas tankers arrive just in time to ensure a continuing supply, and the ships bearing foodstuffs unloading at ports around the country were complementing the policy changes introduced under emergency legislation to keep the shelves in the shops and supermarkets stocked with food.

The population had accepted that it was not the government's fault and as one supported and complied with the new laws and regulations.

Experts mused why. The biggest factor was that food, albeit sometimes different to what they were used to, was still reaching the shelves. Some said it was deeply ingrained into the British psyche, that as an island nation they were more independently minded and willing to accept change and adapt to different circumstances. It may have not been the most accurate analogy, but it was referred to as the 'Dunkirk Spirit,' where the United Kingdom had singularly faced the Third Reich as it had swept through Europe, leaving them the lone opposition to tyranny and oppression. The media played a large part in fueling national pride. After initially broadcasting and printing sensationalist stories about starvation and public unrest they had eventually grasped the concept, following some very angry and curt communications from the government, that they could play a role in helping the country instead of gleefully reporting on its demise.

All outlets then tried to outdo each other on who was the most patriotic. Though much had changed as a country since those dark days, the stubbornness and backbone of the nation was still there. The population was in it together and they would work collectively to get through the crisis that had so nearly consumed them.

The problem was news still travelled across borders. Appeals for help from all European countries had been politely but firmly refused. They barely had enough supplies for their own needs and could ill afford to offer any to others, no matter how desperate their needs were.

Ordinary citizens of Europe soon learned that the UK was still receiving food. The first act the UK had done was to close its borders. Only authorized flights were allowed to land, and the Royal Air Force patrolled the skies, attempting to turn back the rising volume of private aircraft, as those in Europe lucky enough or wealthy enough either flew their own or hired aircraft and tried to break through the cordon.

The Channel Tunnel was closed to all trains and guarded by a garrison of soldiers behind huge lumps of steel-reinforced concrete to bar the way; cross-Channel ferries that transported the bulk of the people and goods were impounded.

The most difficult task was to patrol the seas. Thousands of boats, both pleasure and commercial, left from hundreds of European ports filled with desperate refugees. When the Royal Navy attempted to stop these boats entering UK waters the situation became critical. Firing across the bows of most was enough to persuade them to give up and turn around. Some though persevered. Despite orders for no vessel to be allowed to pass, it proved impossible for captains and commanders to order their crews to fire upon boats containing women and children.

If possible, they were shepherded to a port where the passengers were detained, their boats confiscated, and they were flown back to Europe on military transport planes. Many, though, did get through and the coastline became littered with boats, beached or wallowing in the shallows as they were abandoned, their passengers fleeing inland.

It was hard for these people to hide for long if they had nowhere to go. A phoneline set up was continually inundated with calls from people reporting illegal refugees. Many enterprising coastal communities saw an immediate benefit in all these abandoned craft and hundreds were claimed under salvage law. Estuaries and harbors filled as locals filed their claims, patiently waiting for the global crisis to end and the award courts to reconvene for them to realize the unexpected windfall they hoped would be coming their way.

European navies wanting to protect their own citizens did try to escort some of the boats. Here the rules changed. The Royal

Navy may allow a private craft filled with women and children to get through, but there was no way they were going to allow a foreign naval vessel to enter their territorial waters in breach of the clear warning they had issued to all nations.

Warships postured against each other across narrow gaps of sea. Insults were exchanged, but conflict was mainly avoided as restraint was shown by both sides. The European naval commanders were unwilling to test the resolve of the British who, they had been briefed, had orders to open fire if necessary.

In a few cases, fire was exchanged, as frustration got the better of a few hotheads. Ships were damaged, and a few sailors were killed or injured, but all-out battle was avoided for the time being. The main battle ground so far was the furious diplomatic exchanges, as protests were lodged about British actions. The British Ambassadors and diplomats, for once, had a clear non-negotiable position to stand by. Most were actually enjoying the unusual experience of avoiding the niceties and formalities of diplomatic conversations.

The message they reinforced, was clear: "Our Borders are closed. Naval vessels that enter our territorial waters may be fired upon. All European citizens who enter British territory will be turned away. If any land on our soil they will be immediately returned without process or appeal."

Adriene sat in her private office with the heads of all three armed forces sitting across the antique table from her. They listened as she finished her seventh call of the day from a European leader beseeching her to help them.

"I am sorry, Mister President, I don't know how many other ways I can tell you, and yet you still do not seem to understand: we, as a nation, are unable to offer you any assistance. My ministers have repeatedly responded to similar requests from yours with the same result. A personal phone call will unfortunately not change our stance."

She pulled the phone away from her ear, the shouts of the person on the other end of the line clear for the room to hear. She waited for him to finish ranting before responding.

Her voice full of steel, she spoke slowly and clearly. "I'm sorry you feel that way. Maybe if you had not kowtowed to the Chinese in the first place and put your own greed above everything, then you wouldn't be in this situation. Now I must go, we have a war to fight."

She slammed the receiver down and looked at the men sitting in front of her. "Sorry about that, gentlemen," she said formally, in contrast to her angry outburst. "The one thing that irks me is that is the umpteenth call I have had today demanding, not asking, for help. But not one of them has said 'we' or 'us' as in Europe as a whole. It has all been about them and their country. Which I obviously know is their main concern, but I get the feeling if any help was offered, they would rather it be kept quiet and not broadcast widely to save them having to share it with their European cousins. Now Admiral, Air Chief Marshall and last but by no means least General, let us discuss the way forward. Can we cover the domestic situation first please?"

The admiral, who was head of the Royal Navy, spoke first. "We are stretched, but we are dissuading most from entering our waters, ma'am. Some craft are unavoidably getting through, but the numbers are acceptable and as we know, most who land are being detained and returned.

"I have been in constant contact with my European equivalents and hopefully the few skirmishes we have had will not reoccur. They are under incredible pressure from their political leaders. They are facing mass desertions and one confided in me about the worry of a coup as their domestic situation is unravelling fast and elements within the military are getting frustrated about governmental incompetence. All in all, we are currently coping. As people get more desperate, though, the situation could change fast."

"Thank you, Admiral. Air Chief Marshall?"

"Similar report, ma'am. We are turning most away, and I believe those that get through are detained and returned. Our repatriation flights to Germany are being harassed by the Luftwaffe, but as they contain civilians, they are nothing more than an annoyance at the current time. No foreign air forces have tried to enter our airspace yet. We will remain on full alert with our airborne and ground monitoring stations operating a combat level of operation until ordered otherwise."

"Thank you, Air Chief Marshall. General?"

"All Army Reserve Soldiers and Regular Reservists have been called for duty. We are using them as our main coastal patrol force, deploying them mainly across the south and east coast to assist local law enforcement in their duties.

"All regular forces are on full alert and are ready to be deployed wherever needed. This level of activation is unprecedented though, ma'am, and logistics are proving to be problematic, but we are working hard to solve the issues. I am confident that soon we will have what we need, where we need, when we need it."

"Thank you, gentlemen. Can we look further afield now? General, can you convey my thanks to all in the SAS for their key part in the mission to rescue the scientists. I believe a major has been put forward for both a Victoria Cross by his commanding officer and a Medal of Honor by the Americans. I have read the after-action report and frankly I can see why. I know it is insignificant to what is going on, but I do hope the hierarchy does not see fit to delay or quash it."

She looked at the general pointedly. He nodded in reply. He would ensure the award process would not get bogged down before it reached the Secretary of Defense's desk for it to be then laid before the Monarch for approval.

"Please tell me how the American plans are progressing."

"Ma'am, thank you, I will pass the message. The SAS are back in Gander after their mission. The scientists have been transferred to facilities inside Canada where they are continuing their work. Apparently, President Madeline Tanner is still very much involved with the resistance in Texas. Plans are being made to evac her to somewhere safer, but she is insisting she will not leave American soil. For security reasons they are being tight-lipped about where they plan to locate her. The two guard regiments are beginning to deploy, initially to Gander and then to wherever is required. Two regiments are only a small fraction of what will be required to mount a serious and sustained attack on the Chinese. The Americans do understand that with our potential domestic situation it is all we dare send and are grateful nonetheless." The general paused again, clearing his throat to give him time to phrase his next words.

"Currently, they are having communication issues due to some new anti-radio missile the Chinese have deployed. It is slowing the organization process down somewhat. The last I heard they are trying to organize the militias still active around the country to get them to band together and neutralize this threat under some kind of centralized command structure. I will update you when I know more on that. The US, Russian, Canadian, and UK coalitions' command structure has been agreed and is being set up.

The scale of the mission is, as you well know, of monumental proportions. The Chinese have, through some masterstroke of planning and organization, got troops in strength in all states. More are still arriving by sea and air although I believe that door will be closed soon—"

Adriene interrupted him, picking up some papers from her desk. "Yes, I have just received an intelligence update from General Welch. The naval action in the Pacific has pushed the Chinese fleet back toward the coast. Most of their submarines have been sunk and many ships damaged. They are out of the fight for now. The coalition navies are continuing a harassing action to keep them contained whilst they move the bulk of their forces into position. The third fleet leaving Chinese and Korean ports is being allowed to steam out of range of aircover where it will meet the blocking force of submarines somewhere in the mid Pacific."

She looked at the paper in her hand.

"General Welch seems to be enjoying the lack of formality he is now using to expedite communications. I will read verbatim this section, as I suspect it might amuse you. 'Once the bastards cross the dateline, the Communist cocksuckers will be blown straight back to Uncle Mao.'"

She waited for the chuckling to stop.

"The report goes on to say they are beginning to target the passenger planes ferrying soldiers. A general aviation warning is being broadcast warning that any aircraft originating from either

China or North Korea and tracked heading east will be targeted without contact or notice. So yes, I believe that door is being closed. Admiral, is our aircraft carrier in position?"

"Yes, ma'am. The Queen Elizabeth and its accompanying ships are coordinating with elements of the Russian Black Sea fleet and the US carrier fleet from the Persian Gulf. The east coast of the US is now closed to all shipping and aircraft. Very little activity is being reported and they are positioning themselves for when the plans for the next stage have been finalized."

She looked at the head of the Royal Air Force. "How is the repositioning of our aircraft progressing?"

"Ma'am, the Tornado squadrons have arrived in Canada and we are setting up the logistics to support them for extended operations. Initially they will support the Canadians and Russians in the anti-air operation and then will change to a ground combat role. The one positive note is it seems the Chinese have not committed any of their own fighter planes. It would seem they were relying on their bombing campaign followed up by their ground forces to gain control of all US air bases and assets. This they have achieved, but it does leave them potentially vulnerable to air attack. The issue we have is the task is large and the combined number of aircraft is relatively small. The logistics guys think there are not enough missiles stored to complete the job. Resources will have to be husbanded carefully to ensure we complete the task before the cupboard runs bare."

The telephone rang on the desk. She glanced at it in annoyance before picking up the receiver, speaking briefly before disconnecting the call.

"Gentlemen, could you hold on please I have the Secretary of Defense coming in with an urgent communique. He is asking if you could all remain too."

An aide was just refilling their cups of tea as the Secretary of Defense burst into the room. Everyone present could immediately tell he was not the bearer of good news.

Adriene looked at the expression on his face and said, "Please, Mister Secretary, tell us what is so urgent."

"The Israelis have been in touch and I have had it confirmed by the Saudis. Tehran has gone on the offensive."

The prime minister leaned back in her chair and covered her face with her hands. She stayed immobile for a few seconds as she processed the news. Uncovering her face, she leaned forward, fists clenched and placed them on the desk, asking the question she knew the answer to. "Which direction?"

"Columns of tanks have entered Iraq in force. They are heading towards the major cities. Now the coalition forces have departed there is nothing to stop them. Iraqi regular forces are in full retreat. It's a complete rout."

"How far do you think they will go?"

"Ma'am," he said with an exasperated look on his face, "it's the Iranians. They won't stop until they have the whole Middle East under their control. The Saudis may be able to stop them, they were already mobilizing and are surging forward to protect their borders, but they will not be able to stop them in Iraq. The only other credible force in the region is the Israelis, but again they won't be able to stop them."

He paused and took a deep breath.

"The Israelis have declared that they will go nuclear if their demands to stop and withdraw are not met. I believe the only thing stopping them from already pressing the button is the knowledge the whole Arab world will rise against them if they do."

The general spoke up. "Ma'am, I have discussed this with the Israelis many times, formally and informally. Officially their nuclear arsenal is a deterrent, only to be used to protect their own sovereignty. Unofficially I feel that if they went nuclear then they would perform pre-emptive strikes against everyone they deem a threat. We believe they have enough warheads to lay waste to the entire region. It's anyone's guess how far they feel threats extend. Pakistan has nuclear weapons. We must consider the possibility of them being targeted too.

"For decades the Western world has maintained with greater or lesser degrees of success, stability across that entire region. Now we are no longer there I fear this Iranian attack could be the precursor to a far wider conflict. One which will rage unabated until it comes to its natural conclusion."

She looked at the men in the room.

"Thank you. If you could return and continue your duties, I think I have a few calls to make. Mister Secretary, if you could remain please?"

She pressed a button on her phone and spoke to her secretary. "James. I need General Welch and President Petrov on the phone. *Now*."

CHAPTER
TWENTY-NINE

CHEYENNE MOUNTAIN

"Yes, Prime Minister," said General Welch as he cradled the phone between his shoulder and chin holding a recently received report in a free hand. "I have just received the news too, but to be honest I am not sure what the United States can do about it. We have no working government; our president is currently stuck on a ranch in Texas with only Morse code as a means of communication."

President Petrov also on the conference call joined in. "I agree, General. I will try, but I am not confident of any success. This has been building for years, barely kept in check by all of us as we poured billions in resources into the region trying to position our nations as the main influence. We have all sold them the weapons to kill each other as we played our secret nation-builder games. Now I feel we will pay the price. China must be dealt with first and then we can turn and pick up whatever pieces are left."

"I agree," said the general. "I doubt we can do anything now. Our own domestic situation must take priority over any foreign issues, no matter how serious they may be. We will have to trust that the nations will show restraint and keep any conflict conventional. I can hardly judge other nations contemplating using nuclear weapons when we may have to resort to using them ourselves before this is over."

Adriene sighed with frustration. She knew they were correct. "I understand, gentlemen. We will do whatever we can this end to avoid it escalating. Whilst we are all on the line can you update me on how he plans are progressing?"

General Welch chimed in. "The sea operation continues. We dealt them a blow and the western seaboard is closed to them, but not before they landed the bulk of the second wave of troops and equipment. They still present an incredibly strong force, but if we can keep them contained then we can control their influence. The ground forces are building up and positioning in Canada, but it's numbers we lack. If the Chinese dig in as reports from the ground say they are, the conflict will be a long drawn out, bloody business. Our initial hope is with the militias and ordinary citizens to begin the fight and draw the Chinese into many small localized conflicts which will give us the opportunity to drive south clearing up area by area. The Russians will also start their Siberian operation to take the fight to their own back door timed to cause maximum disruption and confusion. President Petrov, shall I hand over to you?"

In heavily accented English the president spoke. "Thank you, General. Our build up is almost complete. When the time is right, we are confident we can smash through their depleted border defenses and continue south. They question I am being asked by my generals is how far do I want them to go: are we to be an army of liberation or occupation?"

He laughed. "I started this adventure to stop Chinese aggression approaching our own borders, and now I am being asked if we want to bring the whole of China under our wing. The question is how far do *you* want me to go? Because once we start the attack, if it proves successful, it may be difficult to know when to stop."

He let that hang in the air unanswered. "Will the world be happy with Russia extending her influence far beyond the size of everyone else?" he asked. "If we defeat China whilst helping to liberate America, then the whole world order may change. America, with her cities destroyed and military strength decimated will be indebted to us and at the same time powerless to interfere. I am in the curious position of wanting your advice, Mrs. Prime Minister."

The silence was long.

"Mister President," began Adriene carefully. "I can understand and appreciate your position. Without your help the

Chinese will surely succeed, but as you say, if victory is won, what next? The world political map was redrawn when the Chinese launched their first nuclear warhead at a foreign nation. How it ends up is, I suppose, a matter for your conscience. If a regime change can be accomplished in China, then the world will be a better place. When the wealth they have stolen from us all can be redistributed, and the world's trade gets back onto a more even and fair footing, then we will all benefit. We are all intelligent enough to see the dangers of what you can foresee happening. I just hope that we can maintain our current relationship to create a safer world for all our citizens to live in."

"Mister President," interjected General Welch. "I am a mere soldier and whilst I cannot express fully my gratitude to you for the help your country is giving us, I will leave the politics of what follows to others far greater qualified than me," he said deftly. "I will say, though, that when this is all over I would still like to see you as a friend and our two nations working together to rebuild from the ashes of the destruction the Chinese have caused."

"Thank you both," replied Petrov. "You responded as I thought you might. I promise you that Russia as a country will not take advantage to the detriment of the world, the outcome of the war we are fighting." He paused, and with a hint of humor added, "But we are Russians after all. We would expect our compensation to be just and maybe a little weighted in our favor."

PACIFIC OCEAN

Captain Wayne Grant leaned on the rail of the aircraft carrier, looking over the water to the lights showing on the distant coastline of America. Tendrils of smoke from the cigarettes he was chain smoking drifted from his lips as he exhaled slowly.

For the first time in years he felt his life was in danger. He had been their poster boy, the American they had turned and who was willingly betraying his former country. The lifestyle they lavished on him left him wanting for nothing and he was paraded in front of their leaders as proof that their ideology was superior to the accursed American capitalist dream.

But now the situation had changed. The operation was not proceeding as planned. Their fleet had been severely damaged by a well-planned attack from both air and sea. The arrogance and confidence of the commanders had been shattered by volleys of missiles that had inundated the defenses they had thought impregnable.

They had turned on him, accusing him of being a spy and the setbacks they had encountered his responsibility. Stripping him of all privileges, he was banned from all sensitive areas of the ship and was told they were awaiting a decision by the leaders in Beijing for what was to become of him. The sailor who had been his escort was issued with a sidearm and became his guard, following his every movement as he walked aimlessly around the vast vessel.

A flash of light out to sea caught his attention. A distant fire-ball blossomed and slowly fell from the sky until it disappeared from view. He did not need to be told it was a missile strike on an aircraft. The fact the Chinese were not celebrating or even inform-ing the crew what they were, meant only one thing to him.

It was a Chinese airplane being shot down.

He had, when he was first captured, felt disgusted, shameful, and angry at what they were doing to him. As they cleverly ma-nipulated him and pandered to his ego, they turned his feelings around. His own country had abandoned and forgotten him. Piece by piece they turned his anger around and directed it toward the United States until he became a willing collaborator.

He had always known and felt deep down, who and what he had become. Leaning on the rail looking toward the country he had betrayed he reached a decision. One way or another either by Chinese or American hands he knew his life was forfeit.

The one factor he could still alter was his legacy and his con-science. If he met his maker knowing he had tried to right some of the wrongs he had caused, he would let the higher authority judge him. Being involved in the development of some of China's newest secret weapons gave him valuable intelligence. It was why the Chinese could not let him live. His own country on the other hand would let him live for as long as he still had information they could use. There may not be much difference in the timescales, but he wanted to live for as long as possible and that future lay on the distant shore.

He just needed to find a way to lose his guard and make good an escape.

SWALL, CA

Sergeant Eddie Edmunds sat at the table. Against the advice of the town doctor who had ordered bed rest to allow him time to recuperate from the gunshot wound to his arm, he was attending the town meeting.

They had defeated the Chinese, but at a heavy cost. Twenty-five percent of the townsfolk involved in the fighting had been killed or injured.

The local doctor more accustomed to dealing with minor injuries and viruses had performed miracles. Working way beyond his skillset he had operated on and patched up, saving many more lives, the townsfolk he had tended to for decades.

Every town and village around them had, on learning of their uprising, flocked to their cause. Overpowering and killing their small garrisons they had taken their weapons and converged on the town of Swall, where they had all pledged to do whatever was needed to rid their country of the invaders.

Eddie now found himself in command of a small army of Americans. Americans who looked to him for the leadership to continue the fight.

HOLLY RIVER

One thousand miles way Cal sat around another table with militia leaders, a senator, and serving soldiers.

He had been given army surplus clothing to replace his dirty and tattered civilian wear and now felt like he fitted in more with the camouflage and uniforms adorning his companions. Gordon, similarly attired, sat by his side.

Troy had given him and Gordon access to the small armory they were creating from all the weapons they were gathering in the local area.

Gordon had been overjoyed to find an L1A1 SLR rifle, the same version of the one he had used when he was in the Royal Marines, ignoring many more modern rifles he could have chosen, and claimed it for himself. Whilst Cal had also been surprised to find an SA80, the rifle the British Army had upgraded to when the SLR was withdrawn from service. Both rifles leaned against the wall behind them as Senator Gus Howard started the meeting.

"Gentleman and ladies, thank you all for making the difficult journey. You are true Americans who I know will never let this country be ruled by another nation. Now let's decide on how we are going to blow the bastards back into the sea."

TEXAS

Sebastian approached Madeline as she sat on the wide front veranda of the ranch. She had not moved from the spot where she had watched General Liu and Sergeant Cho leave in the general's official car as they began their mission to obtain the virus antidote from right under the Chinese's nose.

She knew getting the sample was critical if they were going to mass produce it and get it to the suffering millions who desperately needed it.

"Madam President, as soon as they return General Welch will send transport to collect it. We have cleared the fences from the pasture land out back. It will be more than long enough for a plane to land and take off. I am instructed to make sure you get on the plane along with the general and once the antidote is safely in Canada, he will ensure you get to your husband at Holly River. He has told me to carry you on board and tie you to the seat if necessary."

Madeline raised her eyebrows and looked at him sharply.

"Can I request you do not make me do that, ma'am."

She laughed. "In that case, Sebastian, I promise to save both our dignities. I take it you will stay here?"

"Yes, Madam President. The transport plane is bringing in with it some reinforcements and supplies. The Russians are going to stay as well. I think with what is being planned, not just across

Texas but the whole country, between all of us we can create enough havoc to make the Chinese wish they had never stepped foot on our land."

To be continued...

ABOUT THE AUTHOR

Chris Harris was born in south Birmingham and proudly declares himself to be a true Brummie, born and bred.

A loyal and enthusiastic member of Chantry Tennis Club, he can frequently be seen demonstrating his talents on (but mainly off) the courts. He is also passionate about supporting the local independent economy, and is a regular at the many local independent pubs and restaurants for which Moseley is rightly famous!

He has a wife, three children and one grandchild, all of whom are very important to him and keep him very busy. His many interests include tennis, skiing, racquet ball, darts, and shooting. He's also been an avid reader throughout his life.

Harris is currently working on a joint project with sci-fi author Devon C Ford, due for release later this year.

Find the author online:

Website: www.chrisharrisauthor.co.uk

Facebook: @chrisharrisauthor

CPSIA information can be obtained
at www.ICGtesting.com
Printed in the USA
BVHW081910220120
570201BV00003B/463